"Look, Cage. I know you're just trying to do your job. But those are my patients dying."

"And it's your reputation on the line," he said without thinking, and saw Ripley's eyes darken further, this time with anger.

"No, Cage—my *patients*. I don't care about anything else right now."

He wished he could explain what he was feeling, but the barriers were still too thick, the walls too high. "I know you're a good doctor, Ripley."

She cocked her head. "Does this mean you want a truce?"

Yes, he wanted a truce with her. He wanted a lifetime. But he'd been a terrible husband once before. He knew better than to try again. So he nodded. "Sure, a truce. Can we start with you giving me a lift home?"

She turned to leave, and he followed her out to the street, gazing at her legs and feeling the hairs on the back of his neck prickle to attention, like there was someone watching.

Someone waiting.

Dear Harlequin Intrigue Reader,

August marks a special month at Harlequin Intrigue as we commemorate our twentieth anniversary! Over the past two decades we've satisfied our devoted readers' diverse appetites with a vast smorgasbord of romantic suspense page-turners. Now, as we look forward to the future, we continue to stand by our promise to deliver thrilling mysteries penned by stellar authors.

As part of our celebration, our much-anticipated new promotion, ECLIPSE, takes flight. With one book planned per month, these stirring Gothic-inspired stories will sweep you into an entrancing landscape of danger, deceit…and desire. Leona Karr sets the stage for mind-bending mystery with debut title, *A Dangerous Inheritance*.

A high-risk undercover assignment turns treacherous when smoldering seduction turns to forbidden love, in *Bulletproof Billionaire* by Mallory Kane, the second installment of NEW ORLEANS CONFIDENTIAL. Then, peril closes in on two torn-apart lovers, in *Midnight Disclosures*— Rita Herron's latest book in her spine-tingling medical research series, NIGHTHAWK ISLAND.

Patricia Rosemoor proves that the fear of the unknown can be a real aphrodisiac in *On the List*—the fourth installment of CLUB UNDERCOVER. Code blue! Patients are mysteriously dropping like flies in Boston General Hospital, and it's a race against time to prevent the killer from striking again, in *Intensive Care* by Jessica Andersen.

To round off an unforgettable month, Jackie Manning returns to the lineup with *Sudden Alliance*—a woman-in-jeopardy tale fraught with nonstop action…and a lethal attraction!

Join in on the festivities by checking out all our selections this month!

Sincerely,

Denise O'Sullivan
Harlequin Intrigue Senior Editor

INTENSIVE CARE
JESSICA ANDERSEN

HARLEQUIN®

TORONTO • NEW YORK • LONDON
AMSTERDAM • PARIS • SYDNEY • HAMBURG
STOCKHOLM • ATHENS • TOKYO • MILAN • MADRID
PRAGUE • WARSAW • BUDAPEST • AUCKLAND

ISBN 0-373-22793-0

INTENSIVE CARE

www.eHarlequin.com

Printed in U.S.A.

ABOUT THE AUTHOR

Though she's tried out professions ranging from cleaning sea lion cages to cloning glaucoma genes, from patent law to training horses, Jessica is happiest when she's combining all these interests with her first love—writing romances. These days she's delighted to be writing full-time on a farm in rural Connecticut that she shares with a small menagerie of animals and a hero named Brian. She hopes you'll visit her at www.JessicaAndersen.com for info on upcoming books, contests and to say "Hi"!

Books by Jessica Andersen

HARLEQUIN INTRIGUE
734—DR. BODYGUARD
762—SECRET WITNESS
793—INTENSIVE CARE

Don't miss any of our special offers. Write to us at the following address for information on our newest releases.

Harlequin Reader Service
U.S.: 3010 Walden Ave., P.O. Box 1325, Buffalo, NY 14269
Canadian: P.O. Box 609, Fort Erie, Ont. L2A 5X3

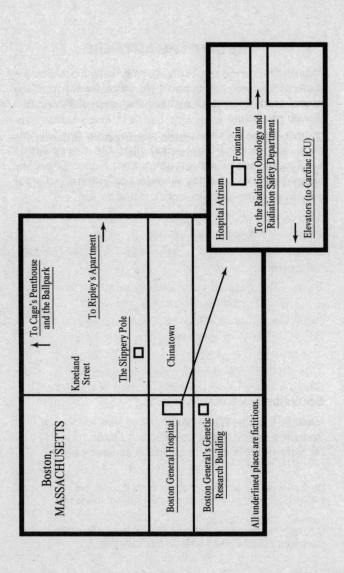

Boston, MASSACHUSETTS

To Cage's Penthouse and the Ballpark

Kneeland Street

To Ripley's Apartment

The Slippery Pole

Chinatown

Boston General Hospital

Boston General's Genetic Research Building

All underlined places are fictitious.

Hospital Atrium

Fountain

To the Radiation Oncology and Radiation Safety Department

Elevators (to Cardiac ICU)

CAST OF CHARACTERS

Ripley Davis—She will do anything to keep her patients safe and her department open, even if it means teaming up with just the sort of man she's vowed to avoid.

Zachary Cage—His mission is protecting patients from unscrupulous doctors like the ones that killed his wife. Will he learn to trust Ripley in time to save her from the serial killer at work in Boston General?

Leo Gabney—The head administrator will do anything to win the Hospital of the Year Award and its ten-million-dollar prize. *Anything.*

Howard Davis—Ripley's father once ran the hospital. Whose side is he on?

Belle—The hospital volunteer loves her patients, but is there a dark side to her angelic behavior?

Whistler—Cage's assistant has the training and the knowledge to murder the patients with injected radioactivity and adrenaline.

Tansy Whitmore—There's something bothering Riley's friend and co-worker, but she'd rather not talk about it.

George Dixon—Cage has replaced him as head of Radiation Safety at the hospital, but Dixon may still be playing a role at the hospital. A sinister one.

To Melissa Jeglinski, for believing in my stories
and helping me grow as a writer.

Chapter One

Ripley Davis stiff-armed the swinging doors that separated Radiation Oncology from Boston General's central atrium and frowned at the unexpected death report in her hand. She'd gone over the case ten times since the day before and it still didn't make any sense.

Ida Mae Harris shouldn't have died.

The failure weighed heavily as she jogged down the spiraling stairs to the lobby, but her schedule left little room for a quiet moment. She had barely enough time to grab a coffee before she was due at another "emergency" Radiation Safety meeting—the second one this month. She'd heard that the head Radiation Safety Nazi had been replaced, but she held little hope for improvement. Rumor had it that the new guy, Zachary Cage, hated doctors.

Great, that was just what Ripley needed.

She didn't have time for a meeting and she didn't have time for a Radiation Safety Officer with an attitude shutting her down for a snap inspection. She was struggling to keep the Radiation Oncology department open as it was, following the last round of budget cuts. But R-ONC—pronounced Ronk—was her life. The patients were her family. The administration couldn't shut her down. They just *couldn't*.

The paperwork in her hand crinkled and Ripley knew they *could* shut her down unless she could defend Ida Mae's death at the inquiry. The sixty-something grand-mother had been scheduled for release. She'd been happy and fit following her treatment. She shouldn't have died.

What had gone wrong?

Ripley shook her head as she turned the corner and strode across the hospital's tiled atrium toward the café. The waterfall fountain burbled to itself, but she wasn't soothed by the sound. Even shorthanded, her depart-ment's survival rate was one of the best in the country. She was up to date with all the new methods and ran a ruthlessly tight ship. The trite explanation she'd been forced to give Ida Mae's husband—*sometimes these things just happen*—was baloney.

She didn't allow *these things* to happen to the patients she cared for, agonized over. She was determined to fig-ure out why Ida Mae had died.

Ripley was halfway across the atrium when she heard running footsteps and her brain fired *emergency!* But be-fore she could spin around to see what was wrong, a hot, sweaty body hit her from behind, and a man bellowed, "You killed my wife!"

She staggered forward with a shriek as the focused re-sponse of a doctor fragmented to sheer feminine terror. She fell to her knees beneath her attacker's weight and smelled old, sour whiskey and unwashed man. Her shock was instant and complete. Paralyzing.

"You killed her!"

Half sitting on the cold tiles, Ripley struggled to face him. "Wait! Wait, I didn't kill anyone, I didn't—" She broke off when she recognized the rumpled, teary man towering above her.

It was Ida Mae Harris's husband. He'd brought flowers every day during visiting hours.

His mouth worked. Grief etched the deep grooves of his face. "She was fine, you said. She was coming home today." He held out a glass rose, one of the many trinkets sold in the hospital gift store. "Our fiftieth anniversary was next week. I bought her a flower."

A tear tracked across one wrinkled cheek as he snapped the glass rose in two with a vicious, violent motion. He pointed the stem toward Ripley. Light glinted off the wickedly pointed end and a manic rage sparked in his eyes. Alcohol fueled the flames to a blast that burned through her chest. "Now Ida Mae is dead. *You killed her!*"

Ripley struggled to her knees and held out both hands, barely aware of the gaping onlookers and the sound of the fountain behind her. Fear coiled hard and hot in her stomach. She saw the hands shake and was only dimly aware they belonged to her. *No!* she wanted to shout. *I didn't kill her! My patients are my life. They're my family, don't you understand?*

But he was beyond understanding. So she tried to soothe. Tried to defuse, saying, "Mr. Harris. Losing your wife is a terrible, terrible thing, but this won't make it any better."

He'd seemed calm when she had called to break the news of Ida Mae's death. But Ripley knew shock—and anger—could be delayed. And intense.

When another tear creased his cheek to join the first,

Ripley thought she might be getting through. She rose to her feet and held out a trembling hand, palm up, and tried to steady the quiver in her voice. Tried to hold back her own scared tears when she said, "Give me the piece of glass, Mr. Harris. Ida Mae wouldn't have wanted you to do this."

It was the wrong thing to say.

"Ida Mae didn't want to die!" the big man roared. He brought the makeshift knife up and leapt on Ripley with a snarl on his lips and fierce grief in his eyes.

The glass stem swept down in a glittering arc and chaos erupted.

A woman screamed. A nearby display of children's watercolors crashed to the floor, overturned by the stranger who'd hidden behind it. Ripley lurched away from Mr. Harris, twisted and fell to the ground as the stranger charged across the tiles, grabbed Harris, and hurled him into the fountain.

Water smacked onto the tile floor and the onlookers shrieked.

There was another enormous splash as Ripley's dark savior followed his combatant into the fountain. She struggled to her feet in time to see the man haul Harris up by his collar, punch him hard and drop the suddenly limp figure back into the water.

And the world stilled. Silenced. Even the fountain seemed muted. And Ripley stared as two pieces of information battled for control of her conscious mind.

She was safe. And the stranger was magnificent.

Breathing hard, six-foot-two inches of rugged male glared down into the roiling fountain with water sheeting down behind him. His long nose and heavy brow made his profile more fierce than handsome, and across the distance that separated them, she couldn't tell what color his eyes were. They just looked…black.

The wet material of his cotton shirt and dress pants clung like a lover to the tight bulges of his biceps and the long muscles of his thighs and calves. Ripley's mouth dried to sand when he leaned down and hauled Harris out of the water with a filthy curse and those muscles bunched and strained.

Paying no attention to the gathering crowd, the stranger stepped out of the fountain and dumped the now-weeping man on the tiles, leaving him for the uniformed police officers who poured into the atrium with guns drawn, only to find the situation under control.

Then the stranger turned toward Ripley and their eyes locked. A click of connection arced between them like a live wire. She felt a tremble in her thighs and an ache in the empty place between them. It didn't feel like fear. Far from it. How could fear exist side by side with this sensation?

He walked toward her and Ripley was barely aware of the growing hum as the onlookers started talking in loud, excited tones about their own imagined bravery during the dangerous moments.

She saw only *him*. Dark, wet hair clung to his wide brow and the damp shirt hung from his chest like chain mail. He held out his hand. Glass sparkled on his palm.

"I'll take that." The nasal Boston twang jolted Ripley out of her trance, and she looked blankly at the officer who had materialized beside her. When he pointed at the glass rose stem, she shook her head and slid it into the breast pocket of her lab coat, though she couldn't have said why.

The slight bump of a glass thorn pressed through the fabric to touch her skin, and she had to suppress a shiver. The imprint of Harris's hands stung her side and shoulder. She could feel him against her, hot and sweaty and mad with grief. The fine trembles that began in her stomach threatened to work their way out, but Ripley knew she couldn't let them take control.

She had to be a doctor now. She was Ripley Davis, MD. She couldn't be soft. *Davises don't make public scenes,* growled her father's voice in the back of her mind, and the familiar anger helped her push the shakes aside.

She could be a frightened woman later. In private.

Gesturing toward the officers herding witnesses into the coffee shop, she said, "That's not necessary. I won't be pressing charges." She focused on hospital policy. Head Administrator Leo Gabney's policy. It was easier to think of policy than what might have happened if Harris had been a little quicker with the makeshift knife, the other man a little slower with his rescue.

The trembles in her stomach threatened to take over.

"Why the hell not?" The stranger's voice was as dark and fierce as his face. It was steel and smoke and anger, with a hint of softness at the edges. In an insane flash, Ripley wondered what it sounded like first thing in the morning.

How it would sound calling her name.

And why in God's name was she thinking about that? She didn't need a man. Didn't need sex. She was a doctor. She saved lives. She didn't need a man to make her feel whole. That was a weakness, just like love. Like the need for rescue.

It was adrenaline, Ripley decided when the stranger's brows drew together in a scowl that she felt all the way to her core. That's all it was. Adrenaline and the shaky knowledge that he'd saved her life.

She couldn't remember the last time a man had thought to rescue her from anything.

Fighting to keep her voice steady, she said, "Mr. Harris needs compassion more than he needs jail time." She nodded toward the new widower, who was sobbing brokenly into his hands as a white-coated ER attending crouched down beside him and officers hovered above.

She could barely make out Harris's words over the growing din. "Ida Mae. The phone call. Dr. Davis killed Ida Mae."

Ripley closed her eyes. *These things happen,* she'd said over the phone when she told him his wife's heart had stopped without warning. Cheap words. The disbelief in his voice had wounded her, because she had barely believed it herself. His sobs tore at her now.

She had failed her patient. Her department.

Herself.

The stranger spat a curse. "He could have killed you! What kind of hospital policy is that? What kind of safety do you people have here? The guy's a nut. He should be punished!"

"He's already been punished," Ripley snapped over Harris's rising howls. "He's lost his wife." Though she didn't believe in happily ever after for herself, it worked for some. It had worked for the Harrises. She thought of the rose stem in her pocket. He'd bought Ida Mae a glass flower to celebrate their fiftieth anniversary. Now he'd spend it alone.

The sting of guilt pierced like a thorn.

The stranger snarled, "That's bull and you know it. Grief doesn't give a man the right to hurt other people."

"Give it up, pal," the officer suggested. "We get these calls every few months. Boston General won't press charges and we've never had anyone seriously hurt. For better or worse, their system seems to work. Now, if I could have your names for my report, I'll get out of your hair."

Ripley gave her name and department. The stranger clenched his jaw when she mentioned Radiation Oncology, but he merely glared at the officer. "My name is Zachary Cage. I think this is bull, I'm soaking wet and I'm late for a meeting." With a final glance at Ripley, he stalked away, dripping.

That was the new Radiation Safety Officer? Ripley stared at him in disbelief. The rumors had been right on about his attitude, but they hadn't said he was gorgeous.

"Hell," she muttered, and lifted a hand to brush the hair away from her face. That was when she noticed the hand was still shaking. Her whole body was shaking. And she was going to throw up.

If you must fall apart, do it someplace private, Howard Davis's stern voice said in her mind. *Davises must never be weak in public. Never.*

She was halfway across the atrium on her way to the ladies' room when she saw the ER attending give Harris a sedative jab in the upper arm. The weeping man's voice abruptly rose above the atrium din. "The voice on the phone said Dr. Davis killed my wife!" Then he slumped to the floor, unconscious.

Ripley made it to the bathroom, barely. But it was a long time before she stopped shaking.

"JUST WHAT I NEED. Another damn doctor trying to save her own hide. Typical. Well, we'll see about that, won't we?" Cage yanked the warm-up pants out of his gym bag and dragged them over his clammy legs. He cursed when his bad shoulder protested. The surgeons had repaired the joint as well as they could, but the ligaments just weren't strong enough for underwater wrestling matches.

"What's that, boss?" Whistler stuck his head around the corner but kept his butt firmly planted in the computer chair lest he lose the rhythm of his solitaire game.

"Nothing. Come on, we're late for the meeting."

"You wearing that?"

Cage scowled down at the faded baseball jersey, warm-up pants and scuffed sneakers. "Not much choice, is there? My work clothes are soaked. Come on."

His nominal assistant obediently tagged along to the meeting Head Administrator Leo Gabney had set up.

"Why the hell won't the hospital prosecute that guy?" Cage snarled. "He attacked one of your doctors with broken glass, for God's sake." He had told Whistler the bare bones of the story. The radiation tech, twentyish and faintly geeky, had barely batted an eyelash. Then again, Whistler hadn't reacted to much yet, except to offer a small grin when Leo Gabney had announced that Cage was replacing George Dixon as Radiation Safety Officer.

The other five members of the team hadn't been as kind. Two had rolled their eyes, one had made a pointed reference to the failed Albany Memorial lawsuit, and the others hadn't bothered to look up from their card game. Cage had considered firing all of them on the spot.

The day had gone downhill from there, culminating in him stumbling upon a woman being held at knifepoint in the hospital lobby. He could still feel the echo of rage. Though Cage knew exactly how the widower felt, there was no excuse for physically harming a woman.

Even if she *was* a doctor.

"If the guy freaked out because his wife died unexpectedly, they'll hush it up," Whistler said with a sidelong glance.

"Why is that?"

"The administration doesn't want a malpractice suit. They're bad for business and for BoGen's chances at Hospital of the Year."

Cage stiffened, and when the memory tried to come, he stuffed it deep down, hidden where it belonged. He growled, "*Malpractice* my ass. Doctors shouldn't 'practice' on anyone. They should know what the hell they're doing before they start mucking around."

Whistler shrugged. "Don't see much of it here. Boston General has an excellent record. The administration has seen to it, one way or another." He pushed open the door to the Radiation Oncology conference room and gestured Cage through.

"You're late." Head Administrator Leo Gabney pounced just inside the conference room. His scowl lacked some of its intended punch because he barely topped five-foot-six. "And what the hell are you wearing?"

Cage brushed past him. "Long story. But for the record, your security sucks."

"Lucky for you, our security isn't your problem. You'll adjust to the way we do things here soon enough." Gabney shooed Cage up to the front of the room. "Let's get on with it, the natives are restless."

That was an understatement, Cage decided as he took the podium. Fifty or so faces stared at him with varying degrees of annoyance, anger and downright hostility. Nothing unexpected. A few coffee-shop conversations and a scan of the files had shown him that his predecessor had been neither well liked nor particularly effective. It seemed that George Dixon had been more interested in women than radiation safety—whether or not the women returned his affections.

Well, Cage thought, the female population at Boston General was in no danger from him. His priority was the job. Period.

But as he adjusted the microphone to chin height and scanned the room, an unfamiliar tingling skittered through Cage's chest, and he couldn't help glancing at the only face that reflected something other than hostility.

She was here.

The woman hadn't been far from his mind, he realized, since the incident in the atrium. She'd brushed it off and hidden behind hospital policy, but he had saved her life and they both knew it. The adrenaline still thrummed through his veins as he peered past the podium and focused on her face.

Dr. Ripley Davis. The statistics in her personnel file hadn't prepared him for that first meeting. Hadn't prepared him to see her as a woman instead of a doctor. A suspect.

In those first few seconds, he'd seen only a beautiful woman with dark, springy curls fastened behind her head, a few left free to brush her jaw and long, elegant neck. The moment their eyes had met, the water he'd been standing in hadn't felt cold anymore. Neither had his body.

It had been a long time since sex had been a part of his vocabulary; even the need for it had been burned out of him. But desire had flowed through him then, as it flowed through him now when their eyes locked in the auditorium and the electricity surged again.

Dr. Ripley Davis. Radiation Oncology. He didn't trust R-ONCs as far as he could pitch them, and he'd already heard rumors of suspicious doings in her department. His investigation was already underway. The fact that she was a beautiful woman shouldn't matter one bit.

It *wouldn't* matter, he told himself firmly. If she was responsible for the hidden radioactive material Dixon had supposedly found in the R-ONC broom closet, Cage would bring Dr. Davis down and be glad of it. He had no patience for sloppy doctors. Especially R-ONCs. And it was beyond unacceptable for unlogged radioactive materials to be scattered throughout the hospital.

Cursing the rev of his body when she smiled tentatively and mouthed, "Thank you," Cage gritted his teeth and glared out at the rest of the assembly. He could deal with their animosity more easily than he could deal with Ripley Davis's smile.

"Attention. Everyone, please!" The Head Administrator waved the crowd to silence. "As you know," Gabney began, "the final ballots for Hospital of the Year will be cast at the end of the week, and Boston General is up for the title and the ten-million-dollar grant. This money would not only go far in easing our recent budget concerns, it would also fund the new Gabney Children's Wing." There was little reaction from the room, but the administrator beamed and nodded as though there had been a standing ovation. "Now, as part of my continued commitment to improving Boston General, I'd like to introduce Zachary Cage, who is replacing George Dixon as Radiation Safety Officer."

There was a quick, speculative buzz, but it died when Cage cleared his throat and leaned toward the microphone. "I know there have been complaints about fines levied by the previous RSO, and I promise to look into those incidents."

There were a few nods and a faint smile or two. These were wiped clean as Cage continued, "But…the radiation safety here is a joke. You know it, and I know it. I intend to bring each and every doctor in this hospital back into strict accordance with federal radiation safety guidelines. There will be no exceptions, no allowances. You will comply or you will be shut down until the guidelines are met." An angry hum skittered through the crowd and Cage saw Leo frown. Undaunted, he barked, "Radioactivity is not a toy, ladies and gentlemen. It is a weapon."

A quick memory of angry red burns on soft skin had his stomach clenching. He glanced down at the notes he didn't need and ignored the hands that shot up around the room. He ignored the chocolate-brown eyes he could feel on his face like a touch and tried to imagine wounded blue ones in their place.

Heather. He was doing this for Heather. He hadn't been able to save her. Hadn't been able to punish her killers. But he could make the hospitals safer for other women. For other men's wives. The widower's cry echoed in his head. *Dr. Davis killed my wife!*

Cage leaned forward into the microphone and made the final pronouncement, the one that was likely to be the most unpopular. "I will be performing a full audit of your radiation use for the last two years, starting in the labs with the most recent fines and infractions." He glanced up and was caught in her eyes. The sudden angry babble faded into the background when he saw the surprise on her face.

And the sudden flash of…worry?

He glanced down at the unnecessary notes again, needing to sever the contact. "My team and I will start our audit tomorrow." He paused and his eyes found Ripley Davis again. It was as though he was speaking only to her. "We'll begin with Radiation Oncology."

This time, the fear was unmistakable and Cage felt an unaccountable thread of disappointment knife through him. Ripley Davis had something to hide.

She was just like all the others.

The meeting wound down quickly after that. Cage saw Dr. Davis slide from her seat as he opened the floor to questions, but she didn't meet his eyes. She hurried from the room while he answered a query about waste containment systems and Cage had a sudden, mad impulse to follow her.

As quickly as he could, he turned the microphone over

to the Head Administrator and walked to the door. There was no sign of her in the hallway. Gabney droned in the background, "I will be personally overseeing the public affairs events scheduled over the next two weeks as the Hospital of the Year voting draws near…"

Cage slipped out of the conference room and headed for the Radiation Safety office, intent on rereading her personnel file. Ripley Davis had piqued his interest. Not because of the way she looked, or because of how she'd handled the situation in the atrium, he assured himself, but because she was a doctor. A R-ONC. And because George Dixon had told several people about finding a jar of radioactive material in the R-ONC broom closet. Unlabeled. Unshielded. Unauthorized.

Unacceptable.

Now it was Cage's job to figure out where the jar had come from. Where it had gone. And why.

He found the Rad Safety office deserted and he grimaced. Dixon had run a sloppy office in more ways than one. "Those technicians had better step up to the plate, or they'll find themselves looking for new jobs," he muttered into the echoing emptiness.

He crossed to the cardboard box that held his paperwork, pulled out the stack of files he'd requested from personnel, and thumbed through until he reached *Davis, Ripley.* He froze.

That morning, the folder had been thick with commendations and biographical material. But not anymore.

He pulled the now-thin folder from the box and opened it.

The file was empty.

Chapter Two

Ripley spent that night going over Ida Mae Harris's lab workups backward and forward until the notations blurred together. Then she staggered to bed and slept a few hours, plagued by a tangle of waterfalls, hot black eyes and unfamiliar aches. The shrill ring of the alarm was almost a relief, but when she reached her office at Boston General, the tension she'd felt after Harris's attack returned in force.

A book she remembered leaving open to a page on cardiac complications was closed. Her chair, which she usually pushed all the way under the desk, was askew.

Had someone been in her office? She glanced at the door. It had been locked as usual. She shook her head.

She was still rattled from the day before, that was all. She was shaky from being assaulted, and worried by Mr. Harris's strange choice of words. *The voice on the phone said Dr. Davis killed my wife.* Had he meant her phone call when Ida Mae died? It seemed the likeliest answer, but the phrasing bothered Ripley. What if someone else had called Mr. Harris and told him R-ONC was responsible for his wife's death?

She'd be looking at a malpractice suit, and even worse,

it meant that someone in her dwindling department couldn't be trusted.

"He's late."

Ripley jumped, cracked her elbow on the corner of her desk, and swore. It wasn't often that her best friend, Tansy, snuck up on her. Usually, the pretty blonde entered the room with a flourish and an invisible fanfare. Men lit up. Women smiled. Her energy was infectious.

Not today. Ripley grimaced. "You look about how I feel. What's wrong?"

"Nothing important." Tansy's smile barely flattened the frown. A sleepless night was etched in the slump of her shoulders and the dark circles under her eyes. "How are you feeling after yesterday?"

"Jumpy and sore," Ripley replied. "And I know Cage is late."

The new RSO's threatened audit was another reason for her nerves. Though Ripley and her technicians were scrupulous about their radiation practices, Zachary Cage was reputed to be on a mission. And Leo Gabney was looking for an excuse to close the R-ONC department and shuffle their expensive patients elsewhere across the city, where Ripley knew they'd get adequate care.

Adequate, but not exceptional. And though she'd originally taken the R-ONC position to prove to her father that she wasn't going to join him in his cushy private practice, over the years the department had become her baby. Her family.

It was the only family she was likely to have, Ripley knew, and she wasn't about to let the administration, or the new RSO, take it away from her.

"Ida Mae Harris's autopsy is today, you know," Tansy broke the silence, shooting her a sidelong glance.

And there was her biggest worry in a nutshell. She touched the manila folder on her desk. It was all that was left of a sixty-eight-year-old woman who'd been looking forward to a milestone anniversary she would never reach. "Yes, I know."

"They won't find anything that Gabney will be able to use against us." Tansy gave her a one-armed hug. Though she spent much of her time on loan to Hospitals for Humanity—HFH—an international group of doctors who took assignments under the worst of conditions, Tansy worked in R-ONC when she was at home. She understood.

"I almost hope they do find something, you know? At least then we'd have an answer." Ripley shrugged. "It's always better to know than to wonder."

"Well, whatever they find, it wasn't anything R-ONC did wrong. It wasn't anything *you* did wrong." Of anyone in the hospital, only Tansy knew how much Ripley needed to hear the words. Only Tansy knew how insecure the seemingly invincible Dr. Davis was about her work, how much it frightened her to play God.

How much it hurt when she lost a patient. A friend.

Ripley squeezed her eyes shut. "I hope you're right. And I hope the new RSO doesn't cause problems." Her temperature spiked as her mind flashed back to black eyes and the hot whispered promises of her dreams.

Or had that been a nightmare?

"What sort of problems would those be?" The rough rumble came from close behind her, too close, and the sizzle that lanced through her midsection was unmistakable.

Ripley spun and faced the door. Cage. She stifled a curse that he'd walked through the outer office and into the inner sanctum without her realizing it, before she'd been able to prepare herself to see him again.

She didn't want him to know about the autopsy. Didn't want him to know that she couldn't explain Ida Mae's death. Her past experience with Radiation Safety had taught her it was best to tell them as little as possible.

And her own reactions told her it was safest to keep her distance from this RSO in particular. With R-ONC's future uncertain, she couldn't afford the weakness that came with an emotional entanglement.

Her father had taught her that, as well.

Cage's face gave away nothing as they squared off in her doorway, and once again Ripley felt that click of connection. Something primitive flared deep in his black eyes and he held out his hand like a challenge. "We weren't properly introduced yesterday. I'm Cage, the new RSO."

She took the hand and felt her heart kick when his fingers closed over hers. "Dr. Davis." He held on a moment longer than necessary before allowing her to pull away.

"A pleasure," he replied, but a lift of his heavy brow told her it was anything but.

"Though I'm grateful for your help in the atrium yesterday, I'm not thrilled about a full audit. I have patients to treat, and the violations you mentioned were Dixon's way of getting back at me for refusing to date him." A hint of temper seeped into Ripley's voice and she gestured toward the outer office, feeling tired and cranky. Twitchy. Tense. "Never mind. Come on, I'll show you where we keep the radiation logs."

She tried to brush past him, but the RSO didn't budge and she ended up too close, staring up into his dark, dark eyes. A tremble began in her stomach and worked its way out from there. Irritation, she told herself. Nerves.

Lust, whispered her subconscious. *Sexual awareness.*

It took her a long moment to realize that he wasn't gazing into her eyes with mirrored desire. He was focused over her shoulder, staring at Ida Mae's paperwork piled on the corner of her desk. "What is that, your personnel file?"

Ripley spun away and slapped a hand on the pile. "This is confidential patient information, Mr. Cage. Off-limits unless you're a doctor."

Something dangerous flashed in his eyes, but he stepped back and inclined his head. "My apologies. After you, Dr. Davis."

Why had he thought it was her personnel file? Ripley had no idea, just as she had no idea why the outer office suddenly seemed crowded and hot.

Hyperaware of him following close behind, she walked to a padlocked refrigerator, pulled out a green binder and handed it to him. "Here's the main radiation log. It's up to date as of this morning."

Their fingers brushed when he took the rad log. "Of course it is." His voice gave away nothing, but Ripley felt as though he was mocking her. Or perhaps himself. "I would expect nothing less."

With that, he spun on his heel and headed for the treatment rooms that branched off the outer office. In his wake, Ripley stared.

"Wow," said Tansy's voice from the inner office. The blonde crossed the room to stand at Ripley's shoulder and watch Cage walk away.

"Yeah," Ripley agreed. "Wow, what a jerk."

Tansy's lips curved slightly and she glanced at Ripley. "That's not quite what I meant. *That's* who rescued you from Ida Mae's husband?" They watched as Cage crouched down and began copying serial numbers off the linear accelerator in Treatment Room One.

A foul, whiskey-laden breath on the side of her neck. Hard, grabbing fingers. A sweep of glittering glass. Panic. Warm black eyes and cool waterfalls. Ripley shivered and rubbed her arms where goose bumps came to life at the thought. "Yes, but that doesn't make him any less dangerous to R-ONC. You heard him at the meeting. He's on a witch hunt."

They watched him bend over to peer at the electrical hookups. With a fleeting spark of her usual manner, Tansy murmured, "I wouldn't mind being the witch he's hunting for, if you know what I mean." She leveled a telling glance at her friend. "But I get the feeling he's already picked her out."

"Did you just call me a witch?" Ripley deflected the quick jolt with sarcasm, but Tansy's knowing look told her the sparks flying in the little office hadn't been her imagination.

What a time for her libido to wake up. What a poor choice for it to make.

"Just calling it how I see it, Dr. Davis." Then Tansy so-bered. "I'm just glad he was there for you yesterday. When I imagine what might have happened…"

"Let's not think about it right now, okay?" Ripley patted her friend's arm and tried to summon a reassuring smile. "It's over."

Then she remembered Harris's words in the atrium, and thought of her desk chair that morning. The closed files. The subtle disarray. And she wondered.

Was it really over? Or was it just beginning?

FINGERS POUNDING on the keyboard of the linear accelerator, Cage congratulated himself on learning three things in the first two minutes he'd been in the Radiation Oncology department. One, Ripley Davis didn't want him auditing R-ONC. Two, she didn't want him to know about the papers on her desk. And three, she was so goddamn beautiful she made his chest ache.

The first two were no surprise. The third was shocking. Cage had thought all the softer emotions had been burned out of him long ago with a single pencil-thin beam of radiation and a tidal wave of guilt.

"I keep the programs updated." Her voice at his shoulder was a jolt he refused to show, but the buzz of her nearness sliced through him and set up a greedy alarm in his brain.

"So I see." And it was true. She'd upgraded the software every time another glitch in the treatment equipment had come to light. "Too bad it takes people dying for Radcorp to debug these death traps." He slapped the shielding of the linear accelerator with a scowl.

She sucked in a breath on what he thought might have

been a growl. "I think those stories are exaggerated, don't you, Mr. Cage? And let's not forget the hundreds of thousands of patients who are helped each year by radiation treatment."

"But it's okay to forget about the people who died because Radcorp and a group of R-ONCs at Albany Memorial ignored the reports and kept treating patients with a broken accelerator?" Cage's fingers were beginning to hurt from punching the keys so hard. He paused, clenched his fists and blew out a breath. "Never mind. The programs look fine and your fixes are up to date. Where are your disposal logs?"

"I get it." Ripley's voice sharpened and the air between them snapped. "You dislike R-ONCs in general. And here I thought it was me you didn't like. Because let me tell you, Cage, I'm grateful for your help yesterday, but—"

Whatever she'd planned to tell him was lost in a flurry of noise and color from the outer office.

"Dr. Rip, Dr. Rip!" With lots of "vroom-vroom" noises and imaginary squealing tires, a purple-haired girl flew toward the treatment room, pushing a small boy in a hospital-issue wheelchair. They skidded to a halt and the girl's hair slid off her head and landed on the floor.

Ripley and the kids took one look at the purple roadkill and started laughing.

Cage took one look at the girl's naked pink scalp and the fine blue veins beneath, and shuddered.

"Livvy, what are you doing here? I thought you were between treatments. Is everything okay?" Ripley hugged the girl and bent to pick up the purple wig. "Hey, Milo.

What's up?" She didn't touch the boy, who sagged back as though exhausted by the shared laughter. A Boston baseball cap looked ridiculously large on his bald head.

Cage's stomach clenched on the three cups of coffee he'd poured into it that morning. One of the reasons he'd chosen Rad Safety was its distance from the actual patients. He could help them without ever seeing them. Without remembering.

"Belle called my mom and said Milo wasn't feeling so hot." The girl was older than she looked at first, Cage realized as she adjusted the purple wig on her slippery scalp. She was probably in her early teens, though her painful thinness and large eyes made her seem younger. "So a few of us came in for a visit. We were just talking about the game next week, weren't we, Milo?"

The boy in the chair nodded limply. "Yep." The word was no more than a breath, but Ripley didn't seem to notice. Her callousness made Cage think of other doctors. Other times.

She glanced at him and explained, though he hadn't asked. "The Tammy Fund has a box at the ballpark and they give it to a different R-ONC department after each game. The kids love it. We've got tickets for next week."

Cage shrugged. "Baseball's okay."

He felt the damaged ligaments in his pitching arm ache. The pain was duller than the throb in his soul, but both reminded him of a man who'd cared more for his career than his family.

"Do I know you?" The soft question pulled Cage from the memory of broken promises and busted dreams, but he had no answer for the girl. Nor did he take the hand she offered when she said, "I'm Olivia Minton."

"Cage. And no, we haven't met." He backed away on

the pretext of flipping the green binder open and studying an unseen column of numbers.

"Don't worry, kids. He's rude to everyone." Ripley glared at him and herded the children away. "Did you just stop by to say hi, or did you want something?"

"We wanted to say hi," Livvy said staunchly at the same time Milo breathed, "We wanted some markers."

Ripley laughed and the sound zinged through Cage. "Going to tattoo yourselves again?" She crossed to a desk drawer and pulled out a handful of pens. "Just remember, these are the permanent ones we use to mark you for radiation treatment. The ink takes weeks to fade."

Milo cheered softly and clutched the pens in his lap like a prize. Livvy thanked Ripley and cast one long look back at Cage before she pushed Milo out the door, but Cage didn't tell the girl where she'd seen him before.

He was five years, one court battle and a master's degree in Health Physics away from being that man. His love of the game had faltered, leaving behind a need for revenge.

"They're not contagious," Ripley said without preamble as she stalked back over to him, holding a thick binder as if she wanted to smack him with it. "You won't catch cancer from shaking hands." She didn't say *you jerk,* but it was implied.

"Those your wipe logs? Thanks." Ignoring the dig, Cage grabbed the ledger and opened it on the nearest table, though he knew what he'd see. Nothing. He'd already figured he wasn't going to find a single digit out of place in the R-ONC department. He'd bet that every sheet was filled in to the last MilliCurie of radioactive material and the last tenth of a rad of waste. He'd find every bottle of neutralizer filled to the brim and every employee's training up to date.

And he'd bet his job she was hiding something.

He hefted the logbooks and ignored the twinge of protest from his shoulder. "I'll get these back to you when I've gone over everything."

"Fine. Just don't shut me down, okay? I have patients that depend on me." She glanced over and tucked a strand of curly dark hair behind her ear. The gesture was strangely vulnerable. "We do good things here, Cage. We save lives."

Cage didn't say anything, because his answer would have been *you don't save all of them,* and that would never do. Instead, he repeated, "I'll get these back to you when I'm done with them," and escaped out into the hall beyond the R-ONC doors.

Once he was outside her offices, he leaned against a decorative column and concentrated on breathing air that didn't carry a faint hint of her scent. He had to clear his head. He didn't have time to get tied up over a woman. Any woman. Especially a R-ONC.

"You okay, boss?" As seemed to be his habit, Whistler appeared out of nowhere.

"Fine." Cage didn't want to talk about R-ONC, or about the way Ripley Davis made him feel mad and guilty and horny all at once. Nor did he want to talk about the rumors of radioactivity gone astray. He wasn't sure who he could trust in the Rad Safety department yet. If anyone. "Any calls this morning?"

"Nothing exciting or I would've paged you." The

young man shrugged. "A few gray egg deliveries." The radioactive material arrived in lead-lined capsules. It was delivered to Rad Safety, checked in and dispersed to the labs.

Everything was checked and double-checked. There was no radioactivity in the hospital that couldn't be accounted for each and every moment of the day. So where the hell had the nukes supposedly found in the broom closet come from? Cage had no idea, but the concept was unnerving. Since he was working on coffee-shop rumor and speculation, he had no evidence, either.

When he'd brought it up with the Head Administrator, Gabney had stared at him, hard, and prattled on about the Hospital of the Year award. Cage had gotten the message.

Don't rock the boat.

Too bad for Gabney it was Cage's mission in life to do exactly that. Heather had died because a group of doctors hadn't wanted to make waves. Cage had vowed it wouldn't happen again.

The doors to the R-ONC department swung open and there was Ripley Davis, marching across the foyer to the stairs. Cage's head came up. "Here. Take these." He shoved the R-ONC radiation logs at Whistler. "Check them against our databases, but don't worry if you don't find anything. I bet they're up to date."

Whistler's eyes cut from Ripley to Cage and back. "What're you going to do?"

"I'm going to have a little chat with Dr. Davis," Cage said, feeling an unfamiliar tingle of anticipation. "I think she and I have gotten off on the wrong foot."

Whistler snorted. "Good luck. She can be a real hard

case with people who're trying to interfere with R-ONC. Her head tech used to say Dr. Davis treats that department like it's her husband, and the patients like her children."

Cage's eyes followed her figure down the stairs, admiring the long, no-nonsense stride and the gentle sway of hip and hair. He grimaced. *Husband. Children.*

In his experience, doctors gave little value to family.

TANSY WAS LATE for their midmorning coffee break, so Ripley sat alone at the rear of the hospital café with her back to the room and hoped everyone got the hint. She was in no mood for company.

She scowled at her muffin and wished the new Radiation Safety Officer to the devil. It was his fault she felt out of synch today. She was tired because she'd dreamed about him and she was behind schedule because he'd insisted on testing each of the treatment machines separately, though there hadn't been an accelerator-related death in four or five years.

And she was worried because she couldn't help feeling Zachary Cage had seen more than she wanted him to, both in the lab and in her. If he and the Head Administrator ganged up against R-ONC, she'd be out in a minute. Her patients would be farmed out and forgotten, and she'd wind up doing a hundred Pap smears a day in her father's practice.

Ripley bowed her head as tears threatened and the bruises left by Ida Mae's husband throbbed.

"There you are!" The dark, rough voice spoke close at her shoulder for the second time that day, but she didn't give Cage the satisfaction of seeing her flinch. Somehow, she'd known he was there. A hint of electricity in the air, a shadow of heat had warned her of his presence.

"Go away," she muttered as he slid onto the wall bench opposite her, "I'm waiting for someone."

She could meet rude with rude any day.

"I saw Dr. Whitmore in the hall. She asked me to tell you she was on the way to an autopsy and she'd see you at lunch." He grinned, but the motion of his face didn't lighten the darkness of his eyes one bit. He knew very well she didn't want him there. "So I'll keep you company instead."

His legs were so long his knees bumped hers beneath the tiny table, sending a buzz of warmth through her thighs. Her chair was bolted to the floor. She couldn't slide away, and Cage didn't seem in any hurry to move.

"Why should I want your company?" She remembered the look in his eyes when Livvy's favorite wig fell off. Scowling, she tried to scoot away from the warm pressure of the knees bracketing hers.

Cage took a hit of his coffee and grimaced as though it didn't go down quite right. "We both know I won't find anything when I look over those logs."

She slanted him a look as wariness sizzled through her. He was fishing. "Meaning?"

"Meaning that your records are clean and your protocols are up to snuff, yet I think you're hiding something. Care to let me in on it? You can start by telling me about those papers on your desk."

Ripley wrapped her hands around her coffee cup and wished it were his neck. She decided to meet rude with angry. Anger was better than the guilt of knowing she couldn't explain Ida Mae's death. She snapped, "I don't like your tone, Mr. Cage, and I don't like your implication. I—" Her cell phone rang. "Excuse me." She flipped open the slim phone. "Dr. Davis."

"Ripley! You've got to get down to autopsy right now." Tansy's voice was tight with tension and Ripley fought the quick panic as she remembered where her friend had gone.

To oversee Ida Mae's autopsy.

Ripley kept her voice steady, professional, all too aware of the RSO sitting across from her. Aware of the pressure of his knees against hers, the accusation that hung in the air as she said, "I'll be right there. Can you tell me what's wrong?"

"It's Ida Mae." Tansy paused and in the live silence Ripley heard Cage's beeper sound. He looked at the display, cursed and stood just as Tansy said, "The body's radioactive, Rip. She's so hot she's practically glowing."

Chapter Three

"I hope this is Whistler's idea of a joke," Cage muttered as the elevator descended. His beeper read 911C-B110, which translated to "emergency—contamination in room B110." Nukes in the basement? That didn't make any sense.

Aware of two nurses and a civilian sharing the car, he didn't ask about Ripley's phone call, but she was headed down to the basement on the double. The thought that they were bound for the same place bothered him, though he couldn't have said why.

"Coming?" Ripley held the door with obvious impatience. He stepped out into the long, damp hallway, aware of the faint hum beneath his skin, a tingle left over from the intimate press of her knees beneath the café table. He frowned.

This was neither the time nor the place for desire. And it certainly wasn't the right woman.

Still, he moved closer to her side as they strode down the hall. Harris had said something about a phone call, and her file was missing from his desk. His instincts, which he'd learned to heed, gave him a sharp poke, a hint of suspicion. What if Ripley Davis wasn't a sloppy doctor after all?

What if she was in trouble?

His mind rejected the idea, but his heart wasn't so sure. And he'd be damned if he let another woman be hurt while he concentrated on other things.

"Rip!" Tansy Whitmore was waiting in the hall, and Cage thought she looked even worse than she had that morning, when he'd noticed the dark shadows beneath her eyes and the deep grooves beside her mouth. Pretty and blond was one thing. Pretty, blond and haunted was another. It made him wonder just what Dr. Whitmore might be hiding. What she knew. "Ida Mae's body is—"

"Tansy!" Ripley interrupted with a quick look back at Cage. A line had just been drawn with him on one side, the women on the other. Inclining his head in acknowledgement, he opened the door to B110 and gestured them into the autopsy room. He grimaced when the smell hit.

Death, with a pathetic overtone of air freshener.

"Hey, boss." Whistler leaned over a body bag with no apparent regard for the funk in the room or the smear of…something on his shirt. Cage had thought before that his nominal second-in-command was a tad strange. Now he was sure of it.

"What've we got?" He hadn't meant to bark the question, but it echoed in the fetid room and battled with the cheerful hip-hop blatting from a radio sitting high above the metal slabs.

Whistler straightened unhurriedly. "We started the radiation sweeps you ordered down here in the basement. You know, work the hospital from bottom to top?"

Cage noticed that the pathologist and the women were huddled at the end of the room. "You paged me for contamination. Where is it?"

And why the hell was there radiation in the morgue?

Whistler jerked his chin at the body, which had been only partially unzipped from its bag. "Right here. Ida Mae Harris is hotter than a Las Vegas showgirl."

What the—? "Then stand back," Cage snapped. "You're not wearing a protective suit, you idiot." No wonder the others were plastered against the far wall. When Whistler obligingly ambled out of range, Cage said, "Where's she contaminated?"

"Not 'where,' boss." The tech shook his head and shrugged to indicate that he didn't understand it. "She's hot everywhere, and I don't think it's surface contamination." He picked up a portable Geiger counter, cranked it on and waved the wand toward the body bag.

The machine's howl drowned out both the music and Ripley's gasp. Cage looked over at her and their eyes met and held. He saw surprised horror. Confusion. And…guilt? Then she glanced over at her friend, and Cage saw the curtain drop over her emotions.

He'd get no more from Ripley Davis. Her priorities were clear. Herself first, the members of her department second and the hospital third. Then maybe the patients fourth or fifth.

Just like every other R-ONC he'd ever dealt with.

With unaccountable disappointment sliding through him, Cage glanced down at the pathologist's notes. The woman's name jumped out at him. *Ida Mae Harris.*

This was the wife of the man who had attacked Ripley the day before. Coincidence? He thought not. Suddenly, the distraught husband's words in the atrium took on a far more sinister meaning.

Dr. Davis killed my wife.

Cage glanced over at her. It was difficult to see the slender brunette as a killer, but he'd learned the hard way that death in a hospital was not always a simple thing. There were often many players. Many mistakes. In his mind, she slid back from "victim" to "suspect" as he reached for his phone and called the Rad Safety Office. "We need all of you down here, pronto," he barked when one of the techs answered, grouchy at having his card game interrupted. "We need to isolate the morgue, decontaminate everything in it, and dispose of this body."

"You can't do that!"

He glanced over at Ripley. She'd advanced to the center of the room with her hands fisted as though she'd fight him for the body. Her breasts lifted with the force of her agitated breathing, and he fought the elemental sexual awareness that clawed at him when she took a step closer.

He leaned down and had the satisfaction of seeing her eyes widen a fraction, though the surge of heat between them was less satisfying. "Yes, I can and I just did. Dixon may have used the RSO job to harass the female doctors who turned him down for dates, but I'm here to keep this hospital safe. That includes isolating radioactively contaminated items."

Ripley snapped, "That's not an 'item.' It's a woman's body. Her name was Ida Mae Harris, and her husband wants to know why she died. Remember him, Cage? Are you going to tell Harris that he can't bury his wife because she's going to spend the next thirty half-lives in a fifty-five-gallon drum in the subbasement? Are you going to tell him we won't autopsy her because we're afraid of contamination? He doesn't care about any of that. Frankly, I don't care about it, either. I want the autopsy done as quickly as possible."

Why was she arguing for the autopsy? He'd have thought she would want the whole incident buried. Or cremated. It was the surest way to cover a mistake.

What was her angle, then? There had to be one. Doctors didn't do anything without an agenda, but what was hers? Because she was absolutely right. For the good of the patient and the hospital, they'd have to find a way to examine the body without nuking anyone. He frowned, confused.

Whose side was Ripley Davis on?

"What was wrong with Mrs. Harris?" Whistler interrupted, "Besides the obvious."

"Breast cancer," Ripley answered. "She had a small lump removed."

Thinking fast, Cage asked, "What radiation treatment?" Some of the newer methods involved implanting a radioactive seed in place of the tumor. If the seed hadn't been properly removed, it could account for the woman's contamination.

"She'd had two treatments under the A55," Ripley replied, and Cage's heart iced at the reminder of another linear accelerator. Another patient. *Heather.* His wife had gone in for a simple radiation treatment and died mere days later. He barely heard Ripley say, "But that couldn't account for the contamination. The accelerator beams radiation into the body. There's no residual source."

Whistler chimed in from across the room, "And that's not all, boss. There are hot spots all over the room with varying count levels." He grinned at the pathologist, who looked as though she might faint. There was a strange, unsettling fascination in Whistler's expression. "I'll bet they've autopsied radioactive bodies here before and never even knew it."

"OH, GOD. THAT WAS AWFUL." Once she and Tansy were back in the R-ONC inner office, Ripley sank to the sofa and covered her face with her hands. She couldn't believe Ida Mae's body was radioactive. What the hell had gone wrong?

She'd sat and talked with Ida Mae, just as she visited with each of her patients. She waited with them. Agonized with them. Loved them. And now this? It was unthinkable.

"Nothing was…odd about her treatment, right, Ripley?" Reluctant doubt edged Tansy's tone. Just back from an overseas assignment with her partner, she hadn't been in town when Ida Mae had started her treatment.

"It was textbook, Tans. I swear. I have no idea how this could have happened." Ripley dropped her hands and leaned back, staring at the ceiling. "No idea at all. Damn it."

"What about the other spots Whistler found in the morgue?"

That discovery had chilled Ripley to the bone. She

shook her head. "I hope he was wrong. If not, then…" She faltered. If not, it meant radioactive bodies had been processed in the morgue before.

She took a deep breath. R-ONC was her department. Everything that went on inside its walls was her responsibility. Ergo, it was up to her to figure out what had happened to Ida Mae Harris. With a little help from Tansy.

But when she lifted her head to make the suggestion, Ripley saw that her best friend was practically dozing on her feet. She looked terrible. Quick concern rose. "Tansy, you look like you're ready to drop. Why don't you head on home? Better yet, page Dale and let him take you home and put you to bed." Dr. Dale Metcalf, infectious disease specialist, was Tansy's partner on overseas assignments. And her lover. Though Ripley didn't believe in happily ever after for herself, it looked as if Tansy and Dale had a pretty good shot at it.

"We broke up."

"You what!?" Ripley stared at her best friend, finally realizing that the red tint to Tansy's eyes and the hollows in her cheeks weren't all due to her friend's habitual insomnia. There had been a good dose of tears as well. "When? Why?"

"It doesn't matter." When Ripley would've argued, Tansy held up a hand. "Not now, okay? I think you're right about taking the rest of the day off, though. I'll be back on Sunday for rounds."

Ripley nodded, knowing that for all her outward cheerfulness, Tansy had a private streak that ran deep. She'd talk about her problems when she was ready to and not before. "See you Sunday, then." Ripley would simply have to work on Ida Mae's case herself. There had to be a clue in the clinical notes.

"Dr. Rip?" The breathy voice from the doorway had both women turning.

Milo sagged in his wheelchair with a jumble of pens in his lap. At Ripley's wave, the volunteer, Belle, pushed him in and took the markers from the sleepy boy's hands.

"Livvy's gone home, but Milo wanted to return these to you personally. Shall I put them in your office?" Belle was a tiny woman of indeterminate age who had been volunteering at Boston General for many years. When her father had died the year before, leaving her comfortably well-off but alone, she had begun spending more and more time at the hospital. Now, she divided her time amongst her favorite patients and the hospital chapel.

"Thanks, Belle. You can just leave them on my desk. I'll sort them and put them away later."

By the time the volunteer had completed her errand and wheeled Milo back out into the hall, the little boy was fast asleep.

"He worries me," Ripley said to Tansy, thinking that the chemotherapy and radiation treatments were hurting Milo more than they were hurting the cancer. The boy was simply tired, and his family's continued absence wasn't helping Ripley keep his spirits up. If she had a precious child like that…

"You should be more worried about your A55 right now, Dr. Davis." The dark voice was a shock, but it was the touch of his hand on her shoulder that had Ripley jolting and spinning around.

"Cage!" She'd been so caught up in watching Milo

slump toward sick, exhausted sleep that she'd missed both Tansy's escape and the RSO's entrance. That was why her heart was racing, she told herself, not because the imprint of his hand burned her shoulder like fire. Then she processed his words and the heat of surprise shifted quickly to anger, both at his disregard for the child and for his implication. "And why should I worry about the accelerator? You checked it yourself this morning. It's fine."

"A patient that you irradiated is dead, Dr. Davis, and her corpse is contaminated. I think you should worry a great deal."

He shouldn't be so appealing, Ripley thought as her eyes glanced over his stubble-shadowed jaw, when he was threatening her. But for some reason, his antagonism was compelling. Perhaps it was the taint of grief at the back of his eyes. She wondered, not for the first time, what had happened to him. Why did he work in a hospital and hate doctors? Who had he lost, and how had it scarred him so?

Why, thought Ripley to herself with a mental shake, *are you trying to romanticize him when he's being a jerk?*

Aloud, she replied, "Of course I'm worried about Ida Mae's contamination." He had no idea how worried she was, just as he had no idea that Ida Mae shouldn't have died. "But I can't see how the linear accelerator could be involved."

"It's killed before."

The flat pronouncement startled her, as did the menace behind the words. The glimmer of an idea formed in the back of her mind, prompted by the tendril of grief she sensed within him. "True," she said cautiously, "but the last of those lawsuits was settled years ago. The technology's improved and the linear accelerator doesn't leave a source behind. Can you honestly think of a way this machine could cause the sort of Geiger counter reading Whistler was getting off Ida Mae today?"

She had to give him credit. He actually thought about it for a minute before his shoulders relaxed a fraction. "No. I can't."

Ripley blew out a breath. "Which means she wasn't contaminated by her treatment." It was only a minor relief, because that still left two questions. What had killed her, and what had contaminated her?

"Well, in that case," Cage began, "if we agree for the moment that the A55 isn't capable of leaving a radioactive source behind, we have to assume that Mrs. Harris was either fed, injected or washed with something contaminated."

The list was chilling. Ripley suppressed a shiver. "I guess we'll know more tomorrow, once your lab has done some preliminary tests." She switched gears. "You *are* going to allow us to autopsy, right? I mean, the radioactivity didn't kill her, so we need to find out what did."

Cage looked at her sideways. "Worried now? Starting to hear the M-word in the back of your mind?"

It took her a moment before she realized what he was talking about. Malpractice. She bristled. "Contrary to what you think, Cage, not every doctor focuses on covering his or her ass. Some of us are focused on doing the best we can for our patients." She fisted her hands at her hips. "Yes, I'm worried. Damn worried. But radiation poisoning is a slow process, and Ida Mae didn't show any symptoms. The radiation didn't kill her."

Cage made a sound that could have been a growl, could have been a curse, and he spun to pace across the outer office. "So it's no big deal that she was *contaminated*? Since she didn't die from it, we don't need to be upset?"

"That's not what I'm saying at all. Don't put words in my mouth!" Now Ripley was angry, pure and simple. "Do you see me trying to sweep this under the rug? Am I pretending nothing is wrong? No. I care what happened to Ida Mae, and I'm going to figure it out if it kills me."

"Forgive me if I find that hard to believe," he growled, but he wasn't looking at her. He was glaring toward the outer office doors, where the R-ONC label could be read backward through the glass. "You're all the same. Money first, acclaim second, righteousness third and patients somewhere down around tenth or so."

Ripley drew breath to blast him into next week, but something about his profile stopped her. His throat worked once, twice, and his hands balled into fists as though he wanted to lash out, yet the grief etched on his face was that of someone who's been lost for a long, long time.

All of a sudden, he reminded her of Milo.

She crossed the room and touched his shoulder. "Whatever happened to you, Cage, I'm sorry. Maybe you have good reason for thinking this way, but it's not fair. I'm a good doctor. I'm not in it for the money or the fame. I'm here to help people. You shouldn't try to blame me for that or twist my motives. You don't have the right."

He lifted his hand and it hovered for a moment above hers, until she thought he might return her touch. But then he let his hand fall and stepped away from her.

"I apologize, Dr. Davis." He was talking to the glass door, and she saw the muscles in his jaw bunch and flex as he swallowed hard and straightened to his full height. "That was unprofessional of me, and you're right. We need to work together to figure out what happened with Ida Mae Harris."

"That wasn't quite what I had—"

He interrupted, "If you'll get me a copy of her workup for the radiation treatment, I'll study it tonight."

Ripley wasn't sure what to say. For a moment, she'd thought she'd seen something sad and lonely beneath the fierce brows and black eyes. But it could have been her imagination. The man standing before her looked as though he'd never had a weak moment in his life.

In fact, at that moment Cage reminded Ripley quite strongly of her father—the most angry, domineering, perpetually correct individual on the planet. The comparison quickly killed her moment of pity.

She ground her teeth. "I'll get the paperwork." *And then you can get out of here.*

When he was gone, she sat at her desk for a good five minutes, waiting for her system to level. She imagined steam coming out of her ears, and the mental picture was satisfying. But as anger slowly drained, she was left feeling empty and alone.

The sore spots from Harris's fingers ached down to the bone, and the outer office echoed strangely when footsteps walked past in the hallway. Ripley shivered and heard a muted tinkle from the pocket of her lab coat when the broken glass stem chimed against a pair of pens.

The sound seemed unnaturally loud. Even the vents were shut down.

"I shouldn't have sent Cage away," she said into the quiet. "Being aggravated is better than this." Her words didn't even echo. They seemed to fall dead the moment they left her lips, but there was a slide of answering motion out in the hallway.

"Hello?" Suddenly desperate for the sight of another human being, Ripley stood and walked across the outer office to poke her head into the hallway. "Hello, is there someone out there?"

The corridor was deserted, but the door to the broom closet was ajar.

"Hello?" she called, walking to the closet. "Mr. Frank, are you in there?" The maintenance crew generally worked the late evening shift, but perhaps the janitor was starting early today. Ripley was so thoroughly freaked out by the bad vibes in her office that even the dour old man's company would be a relief.

She peeked inside the storage room, where a small army of cleaning supplies was shelved beside a collection of mops and a hulking floor waxer. The overhead light was on. She stepped inside and said, "Mr. Frank?" though it was obvious that the tiny space was empty. She was turning to leave when a faint hiss and a whiff of something nasty drew her to the far corner. She crouched down and sniffed. Her heart picked up a notch.

"Mr. Frank," she called, readily identifying the odor and its cause. "One of your bottles is leaking!"

The only response was a soft clicking sound and a sudden deadening of the air. Ripley froze. She turned and stared at the door.

It was shut.

The hissing grew louder, and in the light of the single bulb above her head, she saw a cloud of vapor rising from the corner. The smell grew worse. Her eyes watered and the back of her throat started to burn. She grabbed the doorknob and twisted.

It didn't move.

Ripley stared at the knob in disbelief. She rattled it. Numb shock poured through her and she coughed. The bitter air scorched her throat. The pain spurred hot, hard panic.

"Help!" she yelled, "The door shut behind me and there's gas. Let me out." She rattled the knob harder, barely able to see it through a river of tears. She thought she heard a footstep in the hall and yelled louder, "Mr. Frank? Anyone? Open the door!"

She pressed her ear to the wood and heard nothing over the hiss of bubbling chemicals.

Chemicals. She wrapped the lab coat over her face and slitted her eyes against the sting as she crouched down and peered behind the waxing machine. A pair of bottles leaned drunkenly against each other. Drain cleaner spread from one in a garish blue pool. Bleach leaked from the other, and where the two puddles merged, vapor bubbled and hissed.

Chlorine! She had to get out of there. Fast.

Galvanized, yet already weakened by the foul air, Ripley grabbed a broom from the corner and beat the handle against the door. "Help! Help, there's gas in here. Let me out!" She inhaled to yell again and choked.

It hurt to breathe. It hurt to keep her eyes open. It even hurt to beat on the door. Oxygen. She needed oxygen. Ripley crouched down and sucked at the narrow crack beneath the door, but the seal was tight.

Holding the lab coat over her face, she battled back through the thickening fog and tried to nudge the bleach bottle away from the drain cleaner. But the gas had fuddled her coordination. She pushed too hard, and the bottles tipped over. Bleach splashed into the blue puddle and the reaction was instantaneous.

A gout of vapor erupted. Ripley reeled back and fell against the door, sinking to her knees as her strength failed. Blackness crowded her vision as she gave a few feeble whacks at the door and called, "Help me. Somebody, please help me!"

She thought she heard another footstep in the hall.

Then she thought nothing.

Chapter Four

The anger swirled deep inside Cage as he stalked the halls of Boston General. He didn't like the effect Ripley Davis had on him. He didn't like the things she made him remember. Made him want. She wasn't anything like Heather had been, yet he was drawn to her. It didn't seem to matter that she was everything he despised.

He valued honesty. She wasn't telling him the whole truth.

He hated doctors, especially R-ONCs. She was head of the department.

His priority was protecting the patients from doctors. One of her patients was dead. Radioactive. And her biggest priority was saving her own hide.

Just like all the others.

He halted in the middle of the wide elevator lobby. So why was he walking back to Radiation Safety? He should be in R-ONC, questioning her until she broke down and admitted to taking the personnel file off his desk, until she told him everything she knew about Ida Mae Harris and the radioactivity Dixon supposedly found in the broom closet.

He had an ugly suspicion the two were related.

"Damn it." He spun on his heel and marched back the way he'd come. "This time, I'm not leaving until I have some answers."

But when he reached the outer office, Cage found R-ONC deserted. "It's almost five on a Friday." He cursed. "What did I expect? Dedication?"

Noticing that the door to the inner office stood ajar, he crossed the carpeted floor and peered inside. It was empty. Casually glancing back toward the corridor, he eased across the room to her desk, feeling awkward even as he assured himself it was the right thing to do.

He needed to know what she'd been hiding that morning. He needed to see those papers. They weren't on her desk, so he was reaching for the top drawer when he heard a thump out in the hallway. It didn't sound like Ripley Davis's purposeful stride, but he didn't want to be caught rifling through her stuff. Feeling ashamed by his actions, though he couldn't have said why, he walked across the outer office and peered into the hall.

It was deserted. A faint whiff of cleaning solution suggested that the janitor had begun his work for the evening. Satisfied, Cage turned back to the inner office. Another thump brought him up short. This time he thought he heard a voice.

"Help me."

"What the hell?" Adrenaline kicked him into the hall, which was still empty. The corridor was lined with closed doors. Heart pounding, he yelled, "Hello? Does somebody need help?"

There was no response, but the smell of cleaning solvent grew stronger. He wrinkled his nose and glanced over at the R-ONC broom closet, where Dixon had found the jar of radioactive material.

There was a key in the lock.

"Hello? Is someone in there?" The smell was stronger near the door, but there was no answer. Maybe he'd imagined the voice. His heart pounded as he twisted the key and pulled open the door.

Ripley Davis tumbled out at his feet, followed by a cloud of thick, choking air.

Shock poured through him, followed by panic. She wasn't moving. He wasn't even sure she was breathing.

She looked dead.

"Christ!" When he inhaled, the reflexive cough practically tore his throat apart. Choking, he lifted her in his arms and cradled her limp body against his chest. He staggered away from the closet. Away from the poisoned air. "Dr. Davis! Ripley! Can you hear me?" The words were trapped in his burning lungs, but the pressure eased once they were in the fresher air of the outer office.

She felt light in his arms. Too light, as though the life had already drained from her.

He slammed the door shut and lowered her to the floor. He knelt beside her, as close to praying as he'd been for half a decade. Trying not to remember that his prayers had been ignored before.

"Come on, Ripley. Come on, baby, breathe!" His hands shook as he fumbled for his phone. "Come on, damn it. Breathe!"

And she did.

She took a gasping breath. Then another. Then she

started to cough and struggle weakly against him. A spurt of pure relief sizzled through Cage. She was alive.

Barely.

He couldn't even name all the emotions that flooded through him. Wasn't even sure he wanted to. He sagged down beside her and pulled her onto his lap. "You're okay. Just breathe. Take it nice and easy." He soothed her with mindless words as she curled into him. "Easy now. You're okay. I've got you."

He felt an impotent rage build. He'd been tossing her office while she was in dire danger.

With every deadly incident, it became clearer that she needed his protection, not his suspicion.

Too soon, she tried to talk. She gasped, "Call…Haz-Mat," between breaths in a voice as scratchy as raw wool. "Chlorine."

He placed the call, directing the Hazardous Materials crew to the closet and deflecting their questions with a curt, "No, I don't know what the hell happened. Just get down here." He glanced down at Ripley, who was curled against his chest, shaking. His heart constricted. He'd almost been too late. Again. What the hell was going on here? "Hang on. I'll call the ER and get a gurney sent up.

Her sudden grip on his wrist was firm, though she was still shivering with reaction. "No…ER. I'll be…fine." She pushed off his lap and shook her head. "Not…weak in public."

He missed the feel of her against him even as his mind registered the danger in the emotion. He faced her down, saying, "Bull. You were gassed unconscious. You're going to the ER and no arguments." He glared to let her know he was serious.

Finally, she nodded. "Okay." She wiped her cheeks with the back of one hand in a vulnerable, almost child-like sweep, and said, "Thank you. I didn't think anyone was…" She took a breath. "Thank you." When he reached for her, she shifted away. "No. I'm fine. I can hold myself up."

Cage dropped his hand, realizing he'd wanted the contact for himself, and knowing his brain was right in thinking she spelled danger. She was in danger, and she was dangerous. Of all the women he'd met since Heather's death, she was the first one he was attracted to. The first one who might make him lose sight of his purpose. His vow.

His penance.

There was a commotion out in the hall as the gurney arrived on the heels of the HazMat team. Ripley was loaded onto the bed over her protests that she could walk just fine. As they wheeled her away, Cage could hear her say over the rising din in the hallway, "Nobody calls my father, understand? I don't want anyone to know about this."

He hesitated, knowing that meant she'd be alone. Vulnerable. Then he shook his head. She'd be surrounded by people. Nothing could hurt her in the ER.

He hoped.

"Mr. Cage, over here!" One of the HazMat guys waved.

Seeing that the big inspirators were sucking the last of the fumes out of the closet, Cage glanced in. "What have you got?"

"I've got a gassy closet, that's what I've got." The protective-suited figure pointed to the far corner of the little room. "A couple of bottles fell off the shelves and leaked into each other. Add drain cleaner to bleach and poof!" He spread his hands wide. "Instant chlorine gas. Luckily it was contained in this space."

"Dr. Davis was locked in the closet at the time," Cage said, watching the other man's eyes widen.

"No kidding! What was she doing in here? Is she okay?"

"She'll make it," he replied, thinking that he had no idea what she'd been doing in the closet. Now that she was gone, and her presence wasn't distracting him, his thoughts turned in a new direction. A less welcome, more familiar direction. Deception. What if she'd been in the closet hiding more nukes? Or removing them? He hated himself for it, but couldn't set the suspicion aside. "Do you have a Geiger counter with you?"

"Sure." Another suited man handed it over. "But why bother? Chlorine gas isn't radioactive."

No kidding. Cage didn't bother to answer, he simply cranked on the Geiger counter and swept the room.

Nothing. Relief skittered through him, followed by a sense of shame. He'd been searching her desk while she was locked in the closet with poisonous gas. Now he was scanning the closet that had almost been her death, while she was down in the ER. Alone.

If he didn't get his head screwed on straight and figure out whether to protect Ripley or build a case against her, he'd end up doing neither. He didn't think he could bear another death on his conscience.

"How'd she lock herself in?" the first guy asked. "These doors unlock from the inside."

"Not if you leave the key on the other side." Cage fingered the metal object in his pocket. "I'm sure it was an accident."

Three masked faces peered at him in astonishment. "What else would it be?" one asked.

Cage touched the key again, considering. Worrying. He couldn't believe that she'd accidentally locked herself in the closet and knocked over the bottles of cleaner. But what was the alternative? A conspiracy gone awry? A plot against her? None of it made sense. He shook his head. "Never mind. I'll talk to you later. I'm going down to the ER to make sure she's okay."

He had a few questions for Ripley Davis. Then he was going to wait with her in the ER, whether she liked it or not.

Nobody, not even a R-ONC, deserved to stay in the hospital alone.

TWO HOURS LATER, Ripley and Cage were buzzed into Leo Gabney's office. Her throat still stung and her eyes were an odd shade of red, but she knew Cage's arrival had been her salvation. A few minutes more and she'd have been facing serious lung damage. Or worse.

She suppressed a shiver and took a step nearer Cage. She frowned and moved away again, knowing she couldn't afford the weakness. He'd saved her twice in two days, and she was physically drawn to him. But that didn't mean she could count on him. Didn't mean she liked him.

Didn't mean she wanted him.

He was rude. He was afraid of cancer patients. He was the RSO and she was a heartbeat away from losing her department.

And he reminded her of her father.

Besides, Cage had been sending conflicting signals ever since he'd shown up in the ER. Sometimes she had felt protected by his fierce bulk. Other times it seemed as though he thought she'd locked herself in the closet to throw off suspicion. That he thought she'd killed Ida Mae and was trying to cover it up.

He might not be able to make up his mind, Ripley thought, but she had. She didn't need Zachary Cage to protect her. She was just fine on her own.

Except that he's saved you twice in two days. And you liked it when he held you. Unable to deny the truth of it, Ripley ground her teeth as the Head Administrator waved them to chairs facing his ocean-sized desk.

"Dr. Davis. Mr. Cage." Gabney sat down and grew six inches. Rumor had it his desk chair was so tall his feet didn't hit the floor. "What's this I hear about problems in Radiation Oncology?"

"Big problems." Cage rose to his feet and prowled the spacious room like a jungle cat, pausing for a moment in front of the scale model of the Gabney Wing that would be built if, no, *when* Boston General won the ten-million-dollar grant. "Dr. Davis was attacked yesterday by a patient's husband."

Ripley couldn't guess the mood behind Gabney's pudgy face and cool gray eyes. She'd never been able to read the Head Administrator, even the day he'd called her in to tell her R-ONC was next on the downsizing list. The little man had savored the news, knowing it was an underhanded blow at her father, Howard Davis, who had been Gabney's predecessor as Head Administrator. Now he shrugged. "The Harris case is old news, and it's been dealt with."

Startled, she asked, "What do you mean, 'dealt with'?" How could Ida Mae's death have been settled when they still didn't know why she died?

A small smile tugged at the administrator's lips. "We can't have rumors that our head R-ONC killed a patient, now, can we? At least not until the award has been given out." He sniffed and flicked his fingers to indicate that the attack had been a nuisance rather than a real threat to Ripley's life. "The witnesses have been spoken to, and I smoothed things over with Mr. Harris personally, though we may revisit the topic in a few weeks."

The subtext was clear. Gabney needed R-ONC intact for the vote. After that, she was expendable, and so was her department. Damn it! With no local R-ONC openings, she would either have to give in to her father's demands or start over in a new city. A new hospital.

And what of her patients here? She feared some of them, like little Milo, would fall through the cracks and disappear. She couldn't let that happen.

But at the same time, she couldn't ignore Ida Mae's death or the radioactivity in her body. Nor could she ignore Cage, who asked, "What did Mr. Harris say when you spoke to him? Yesterday, he said the voice—"

"What he said is not important, Mr. Cage," Gabney interrupted firmly. "Harris was overwrought and not responsible for his actions. Beyond which, he'd been drinking heavily. He has no recollection of what he said or did."

"Convenient," Cage muttered with a black look at Ripley. She wasn't sure if he was angry with her or the administrator. "But it doesn't change the fact that his wife's body is badly contaminated, nor does it explain the file that disappeared from my desk, or what Dr. Davis was doing in the R-ONC broom closet."

"I didn't touch your desk," she snapped, "and I told you, the broom closet was an accident." Though she was still shaking from her terrifying experience, Ripley couldn't believe it had been deliberate. It was too horrible to contemplate. She'd think of such things later, in private, when she could be afraid. *Weak.* "Mr. Frank left the door open and I went inside to see where the smell was coming from."

She didn't want to remember the fear that had driven her into the hallway in the first place. The sense that she was all alone, or worse, not alone at all.

"Mr. Frank was working on the other side of the building," Cage retorted. "And it wasn't his key in the lock."

"It was an accident," Ripley repeated, not meeting Cage's eyes. She didn't want him to see the doubt there. The fear. The weakness. "What's the alternative, that someone set a trap for me? Be real, Cage. Nobody cares enough to kill me, except maybe Harris, and he's in Psych."

"Of course it was an accident," Leo agreed, though Ripley held no illusions that he cared for her welfare. "Let's be realistic. Nobody locked Dr. Davis in the closet and tried to poison her. Things like that just don't happen at Boston General." His eyes slid over to the scale model of the Gabney Wing, and Ripley could almost hear the words, *and they certainly don't happen the week of the Hospital of the Year vote.*

Cage scowled. "Yet Dixon claimed to have found radioactivity in that same broom closet before he left the RSO's position. Doesn't that strike you as odd?"

"What!?" Ripley surged to her feet. "What the hell are you talking about?" The shout tore at her abused throat, but she was too upset to care. She turned on Gabney. "There were *nukes* found near my department and you didn't tell me about it?" She saw Cage watching her out of the corner of his eye and she snapped, "What? Did you think I put them there? Have I acted surprised enough to convince you I didn't?"

He shrugged. "Perhaps. Or else you're an excellent actress."

"I would never, *ever* do something to endanger my patients, Cage," she hissed. "And that includes misusing radioactivity."

"So why does Ida Mae Harris practically glow?"

"I don't know!" she shouted, then subsided back into her chair when her raspy voice gave out on the last word. "I don't know," she whispered.

"So you say. Which only proves the point that we need official help. This is beyond both of us." Cage slapped a hand on Leo's desk hard enough that the administrator jumped. "I want you to quarantine the morgue, I want Ida Mae Harris's room locked down until I clear it, and I want access to the husband." Cage shot a glance at Ripley. "I want R-ONC shut down, I want a guard assigned to Dr. Davis until further notice, and I want to call the police in to launch an investigation."

There was a beat of silence. Then, surprisingly, a chuckle from the Head Administrator.

"An investigation of what?" Derision laced Gabney's voice. "You have no evidence that there was ever radioactivity in the broom closet because Dixon lost it. And you said yourself that HazMat considers the chlorine gas an accident. Dr. Davis is fine and nothing more needs be said about the matter."

"And Ida Mae Harris's body?" Cage's voice was level.

Gabney shrugged. "Like I said, the husband has been dealt with." His eyes sharpened and he leaned forward and poked a chubby finger at Cage's chest. "Nothing fishy is going on in Boston General, do you hear me? You have no evidence and no case, and I don't want to hear anything more about this. I fired Dixon for gossiping and I'll do the same for you. Just do your job and shut up, Cage. Got it?"

Ripley's stomach twisted and she sagged back in her chair. Gabney didn't care about her safety. He didn't care about the patients' safety. He only cared about the hospital's reputation. Ten million dollars' worth of Boston General's reputation.

The sense of betrayal was keen.

"And if my job includes investigating a radioactively contaminated corpse?" Cage's voice was deadly even.

Gabney twitched a shoulder. "Then by all means, investigate. Quietly." He flicked a glance at Ripley. "Dr. Davis will help you, if she knows what's good for her career. I don't want anyone else involved. The fewer people who know about this, the quieter it will stay. George Dixon taught me that." The Head Administrator leveled a look at Cage, and Ripley suppressed a shiver at the menace in the small man's eyes. "But keep in mind that if you do anything to interfere with the awards vote, your *evidence*—and your jobs—will disappear faster than you can say 'Nuclear Regulatory Board.' Do you understand?"

Cage didn't answer. He simply turned and left the room.

Ripley stared at her boss for a beat. He smiled slightly. "Dr. Davis, I'm willing to overlook a single unexpected death in R-ONC. I'm even prepared to cover a malpractice suit. That is the cost of doing business at Boston General." He leaned forward and leveled a finger at her. "But I will not allow you to interfere with Boston General becoming Hospital of the Year. Remember that when you are *assisting* Cage in his investigation."

The emphasis on the word, and Gabney's raised eyebrow left no misunderstanding. If she foiled Cage's investigation and helped Gabney cover up the radioactive corpse, she could keep R-ONC. If she helped Cage, she could lose her job, her department, and her patients.

But she might save her own life.

Chapter Five

Out in the hallway, Cage cursed the Head Administrator for putting money ahead of the patients' safety. Then he cursed himself for having thought it would be different at this hospital. But just as he'd walked into the courtroom expecting the system to punish the doctors who'd killed his wife, he'd taken the Boston General job at face value.

He should've known better. Idiot.

"I can't believe him." To her credit, Ripley looked furious, though her red-rimmed eyes and rough voice probably owed as much to the chlorine gas. "The Head Administrator is supposed to run the hospital, not hide its problems."

"It usually amounts to the same thing." Cage took a deep breath and leaned against the wall, feeling fatigue hit him all at once. Fatigue, frustration and a dull depression. Why had he thought things would be different? When Ripley yawned, he glanced at his watch and was surprised to see that it was well after 8:00 p.m. "Come on, I'll drive you home."

Surprise, then wariness flickered across her face. "Why?"

Because he didn't believe the broom closet had been an accident. Because the Head Administrator's motivations worried him. Because he didn't know how Ida Mae Harris had died, or why she was radioactive.

And because he didn't want to let Ripley go just yet. Didn't want to go home alone to the newly reopened penthouse he'd once shared with Heather. Depression dragged harder at the thought.

But he didn't say any of these things, because the wiser part of him still didn't trust Ripley. Still insisted that she could be, if not solely responsible for the body's contamination, involved in it—right up to her pretty little neck.

So instead he scowled. "Because Gabney said we should work together. My options for help seemed to be limited to you or nobody."

"Thanks for the vote of confidence." She crossed her arms and glared at him. "I'm no happier with it than you are, Cage, but I'm bound and determined to find out what happened to Ida Mae."

"And why is that?" he shot back. "It seems that your precious job would be safer if you just let it slide. Why the concern?" Was she truly upset for her patient, or was there a deeper, more sinister layer to it?

Her eyes darkened as she marched right up to him and lifted her chin at a haughty angle. "I don't have to explain myself to the RSO, Cage. You should be glad I'm willing to help you when Gabney's made it clear he'd rather we just dropped the subject."

She stuck out her jaw, looked up into his eyes and paused. He knew the moment she realized they were nose to nose, practically kissing close. Her eyes widened fractionally and she sucked in a breath. All the reasons why this couldn't possibly happen fled from Cage's mind as he brushed a dark curl away from her face with a fingertip and felt his heart thunder in response.

"I won't drop it, no matter what Gabney wants," he said, giving in to temptation and touching the springy curl again. "It's too important."

He expected her eyelids to ease shut, as his wanted to, but she remained staring full at him. Seeing too much. Finally, she nodded, firmed her chin and stepped away from him. The single pace seemed to put her miles away. "Then it's settled. We'll investigate Ida Mae's death together."

"Ripley…"

She shook her head, and in a way he was relieved. The two of them together would be too dangerous. Too unwise. Too complicated. She turned and walked away, calling, "Thanks for the offer of a ride, but I've got my car in the garage. See you back here tomorrow morning to get started with our investigation?"

He didn't bother mentioning that the next day was Saturday. It didn't seem important. Cancer and radioactivity didn't take the weekends off. Neither did death.

Or suspicion.

But when she was halfway down the hall, he called, "Be careful, okay?"

Though Gabney was correct that there was no evidence her attacks had been anything but a strange series of events, Cage couldn't escape the nagging worry that they were something else. Something sinister.

She sketched a wave without turning around. He

thought she squared her shoulders. "I'll be fine. See you tomorrow." And she disappeared around the corner, bound for the garage. After debating with himself for less than half a minute, Cage strode after her. It didn't matter if she saw him following her.

He was going to make sure she got home safe whether she liked it or not.

THE ANSWERING MACHINE was blinking when Ripley walked through the door to her first-floor apartment on the edge of Boston. She ignored the machine and collapsed on the couch instead. When Simon jumped in her lap, she gathered the Siamese cross close and buried her face in his fur.

Then, finally, she could let herself fall apart.

The deep shudders started in her aching stomach and radiated outward, clenching her muscles and wracking her torn throat with almost silent sobs that she muffled in the patient cat's fur.

Scared. She had been so scared. She could still smell the gas on her clothes. When she closed her eyes, she could hear the hiss of the chemical reaction and feel the burning suffocation.

And she was alone. So alone. But when she was alone, she could be weak. She could be afraid. That was allowed.

So she curled up in a little ball on the sofa, clicked the television on for background noise, and let herself be afraid.

When a pair of headlights washed through the room a few minutes later, she shot to her feet, still clutching

Simon. *I'll be fine,* she'd told Cage, waving over her shoulder so he couldn't see the fear in her eyes. *See you tomorrow.*

What she'd really wanted to do was beg him to stay with her. Protect her. Be with her.

There had been a moment in the hallway when he'd thought of kissing her. She'd known it, and had even welcomed the idea. But then sanity had reasserted itself. The attraction between them was another sort of weakness. Love was a weakness. Just look at her mother and father. Her mother was weak. Her father, invincible.

Ripley had sworn never to fall into that trap. She wouldn't, *couldn't* let herself want Cage. Need him.

The headlights moved on and she blew out a breath. It was nothing. Just someone passing by on the way to somewhere.

The thought wasn't entirely reassuring.

Tears spent, breath hitching, she reached over and punched the play button on her neglected answering machine. She stroked the sleek line of chocolate fur along Simon's spine as the bruises left by Mr. Harris's fingers throbbed in time with her heartbeat.

The machine beeped to indicate a message, but there was no recording. Just a long moment of silence and the click of a disconnect. Ripley shook off a shiver of nerves and changed the cable channel from a true crime show to a documentary on honeybees.

There was another beep. Another silence and a click. She looked out the darkened window.

The night was too quiet outside her small, ground-floor apartment. She held Simon a little more tightly.

Was that a movement in the shadows outside? She shrank back away from the night.

A sudden ring made her jump. She stared at the phone. What if there was nobody on the other end? It rang again. And again.

Finally, she picked the handset up and answered with a tentative, "Hello?"

"Caroline."

"Father." Relief was immediate and overwhelming. It was so complete that she didn't even remind him she preferred her middle name, though it was part of the war they'd been fighting much of her adult life. Ever since her mother had left. "How are you?"

Howard Davis never wasted time on small talk or other soft, unimportant things. He barked, "I hear there was trouble at the hospital today."

Though he'd left his position as Head Administrator of Boston General for a cushy private practice a few years earlier, Howard had stayed on as the head of the Board of Directors. In addition, he had spies who seemed to do nothing but report on Ripley's existence at the hospital. The problem was, they only ever reported her mistakes.

But for a change, it seemed as though they'd reported something else. Something important. Although she'd ordered the ER attending not to notify her father, Ripley's eyes welled at the thought that he'd found out anyway, and had called to make sure she was okay. His voice touched a young, needy chord within her. She sank down on the couch and curled her legs beneath her as she held the phone to her ear. The darkness outside the window suddenly didn't seem as threatening anymore. Someone cared that she was okay.

"I'm fine, Father, really. But thank you for asking."

"Asking about what?" he snapped. "Don't be silly. You've had an unexpected death, a contaminated body and a crazed husband howling about you killing his wife. I hardly consider that fine, Caroline. Things like this don't reflect well on your mother and I, you know."

The familiar, dismissive tone fell on Ripley's soul like a lead weight and one fat tear crept to her cheek before she dashed the others away. He was talking about the problems in R-ONC. She curled up tighter on the couch and fought to keep her voice from cracking. "Are you aware that I was almost killed by Mr. Harris? And again today in a chlorine spill?"

"I was told the chlorine was nothing, Caroline. An accident. Don't be dramatic. We're talking about important things here. We're talking about your reputation." *And mine,* was the unstated follow-up that buzzed on the line.

Ripley closed her eyes. Why had she thought this time would be any different from the hundred other conversations they'd had before?

Howard Davis was a controlling workaholic whose wife had left him for a grand tour of the world's country clubs, yet Ripley was, and would always be, the embarrassment.

Simon yowled when her fingers tightened on his fur. Tears pressed harder, but she willed them back, refusing to give her father the satisfaction. *Davises must never make scenes.*

"Thank you for your opinion, Father, but none of this concerns you. I'll handle it." She wasn't sure how she was going to fix the mess in R-ONC, but the last thing she needed was her father's interference, which would most likely involve negotiating a severance package with Gabney. "And I don't believe that it should reflect on you— or Mother—one way or the other."

In fact, Ripley doubted Eleanor Davis knew there was trouble at Boston General, or that it involved her daughter. Some doctors' wives took up good works to combat their husbands' long hours and career-mindedness. Others drank.

Ripley's mother played golf. Lots of it.

"Well, you always have been naive, Caroline. What you do reflects on the Davis name, as well as on the reputation of Boston General. But don't worry about it. I'll have a word with Leo and fix everything for you." Ripley could all but feel her father's hand pat her on the head.

She flared. "You'll do nothing of the sort, Father. Do not speak to Leo Gabney on my behalf, do you hear me? This is my life, my problem. I'll take care of it." Her voice rose to a scratchy shriek, "And my name is Ripley!"

As he always did when she spoke to him out of turn, Ripley's father simply ended the conversation. The buzz of the disconnected line rattled in her head like the words she'd heard a thousand times. *We'll speak again when you're ready to be reasonable.*

She swore viciously because she was tired of crying, and because anger felt more powerful than tears. Simon yowled in Siamese sympathy.

The phone rang again. She snatched it up immediately and hissed, "I swear to God if you call me Caroline I'm hanging up this phone and ripping it out of the wall."

There was a pause, then a dark, gravelly voice said, "Okay. I'll keep that in mind."

Ripley's heart sank. At least she thought that's what the fluttery, sick feeling was. "Cage."

He didn't bother with pleasantries either. He simply said, "We've got a problem."

She thought of her father lining up behind Leo to sweep the situation under the rug, whether or not it endangered the patients and the hospital staff. She thought about R-ONC, and the very real possibility that she could lose her job. Then she thought about Mr. Harris sitting on the tile floor of the atrium, sobbing into his hands. *Dr. Davis killed my wife.* She thought about the click of the closet door and the feel of Cage's arms around her when she'd regained consciousness.

The look in his eye when they'd almost kissed in the hallway.

Her voice was dry when she said, "The way I see it, Cage, we've got more than one problem."

"You have no idea," was his laconic response. "Can you come down here?"

Ripley glanced at the digital display on the cable box. It was past ten o'clock. "Down where? You're not still at the hospital, are you?"

"I couldn't relax at my place," he said, and there was something soft and hurting in his voice. "So I came back here. I found something you should see."

Ripley thought about going back to the hospital in the deep darkness, and shivered, though she'd done a thousand night rounds before. Then she stiffened at a noise from outside the window. Simon arched his back and hissed.

It's only the wind, she told herself, *a tree branch or a stray cat.* But she found herself nodding into the phone. "Okay, I'll be there in fifteen."

Before leaving, Ripley arranged to have Simon stay with her upstairs neighbor, who took care of the cat when she was away on business. She couldn't have said why, but she didn't want to leave him in the apartment.

Just in case.

DOWN IN BASEMENT LEVEL ONE, Cage stared at rows of sliding drawers that held samples from a thousand bodies. But he didn't see the neat labels or the gruesome smears and bits. His mind kept showing him implacable gray eyes. His ears echoed with the words, *You have no hard evidence.*

He'd heard those words before, from the judge who'd excused Heather's killers. The words—and the echoes of failure—had driven him out of the penthouse, where he'd been wandering from room to room, looking at old photos of himself and wondering what had happened to the young kid in the baseball uniform.

The ghosts had chased him back to the hospital, where only the ER seemed alive. Everything else was dead, like the bits of preserved flesh surrounding him.

Like his wife.

"Hey, Cage. What have you got?"

He turned and tried to hide his reaction to the sight of Ripley Davis. Tired, rumpled and faintly red-eyed, she was still gorgeous. Her dark hair curled near her face, her narrow hands tucked into her pockets. Ever since he'd followed her practical navy sedan to the outskirts of town and seen that she was safely inside her home, he'd worked to steel himself against the jolt of her voice and the sharp spike of lust he resented her for causing because she wasn't Heather.

If he wanted Ripley, Cage knew, then Heather was truly gone.

Gritting his teeth, he gestured to the workbench where he'd spread out the blood slides and matched them to tissue samples from the same patients. "I thought about the hot spots Whistler found in the morgue. The old bodies are long gone, but every tissue and blood slide that comes through here is archived. I scanned the drawers with the last six months' worth of patients, and I found these."

Their fingers touched when she took the Geiger counter, and Cage endured the flash of heat, praying she couldn't feel it. But he knew from her quick indrawn breath and averted eyes, he wasn't alone in feeling the sizzle of chemistry.

And he wasn't alone in wishing they'd found the spark elsewhere.

"Are they all hot?" Without waiting for his answer, Ripley passed the wand over each of the samples, watching the instrumentation flicker. She answered her own question, "They're contaminated. But most of the readings aren't very strong."

As he watched her separate the slides by tissue type and scan again, Cage silently acknowledged that the basement didn't seem as cold anymore. Didn't seem so quiet. And he hadn't prepared himself for that.

"It's in their blood, isn't it?" After a few more moments of scanning, she straightened and pressed both hands to the small of her back.

"Yeah." The word sounded thick and he cleared his throat, realizing he could smell her natural scent over the funk of chemicals and death. That frustrated him. Angered him. Who was she to be getting under his skin this way? "Not surface contamination or ingestion, which pretty much rules out accidental contact or tainted food."

She gazed down at the fragments of humanity spread out before her. "How many?"

"Four other patients beside Ida Mae, all women. Their bodies are long gone, but the slides are hot as hell, even now." He paused and felt the fury build, though he wasn't sure who it was directed at anymore. He was frustrated, angry, and he wanted to lash out at someone. Something. Patients had died here. These women had been mothers and daughters.

Wives.

"Which department did they come from?" she asked, looking at him, eyes stark in her pale face.

"R-ONC." He handed her the list he'd pulled up from the Pathology computer and wished he could hold her. Wished he could punish her. "They were all your patients."

"*My* patients." She drew a sharp breath and backed up until she bumped into the shield, which rattled at the blow. "No."

He followed and crowded her, glared down at her, wanting to scald her for having a doctor's carelessness while playing God. Wanting to hurt her because she made him need again.

Wanting to hold her despite it all. Damn it.

The anger twisted inside him, mixed with something far more complicated. Cage held on to the anger because it was easier. Safer. "Yes. Your patients. Do you have an explanation for that, *Dr. Davis?* The cause of death listed for all of them was heart failure. Isn't that what Ida Mae died of?" He leaned down until they were practically nose to nose. "Is there something you'd like to share with me?"

Her mouth worked. Her eyes glittered. For a split second, he thought she was going to cry. If she did that, he would feel terrible, because part of him knew she was as bothered by the deaths as he was.

Her lips trembled. Then she kicked him in the shin.

"Ow! Goddammit!" He hopped back a step and she helped him along with a two-handed shove. She advanced toward him with both fists clenched.

"Don't you loom over me, Zachary Cage. And don't yell at me either. I get enough of that from my father." She scowled and poked him in the chest with a finger. "You want to know about Ida Mae? I'll tell you. *I have no idea why she died.* And it bothers the hell out of me. I spent all last night going over her records, trying to find something I missed. And do you know what? I didn't find a damn thing."

"But you knew there was something unusual about her death and you didn't say anything," Cage growled, hating that he inhaled her scent with every breath, but unable to back away. "Covering your ass, doctor?"

"I was being logical," she returned. "Most unexpected deaths have reasonable explanations that we find during autopsy. Sometimes sick people die, Cage." Her words made sense, but he saw the shadows in the back of her eyes and pounced.

"Then why investigate Ida Mae? You know something, don't you?"

"I don't know a thing." She sounded suddenly tired. "But nothing I say is going to convince you. I pulled her records because I care about my patients and I take it personally when they die." She glanced down at the slides spread across the desk. "Very personally. I'll call up these files now and look them over. Maybe there's a problem with one of our protocols. God, I hope not. I don't know what else it could be, though."

Five dead patients. A doctor who had started to investigate on her own. Two near-fatal incidents in two days. The constellation gelled in Cage's mind to a single, horrible suspicion. "What if someone didn't want you looking at Ida Mae's records?" he asked, feeling gut-punched. "What would happen to your investigation if you were injured?" Or dead.

She shuddered and wrapped both arms around herself. "You'd work on it."

He slid an arm around her and rubbed a hand across her back, hoping to warm her. Hoping to soothe himself. The walls seemed to press closer. The rows of cabinets seemed to lean in to listen. "Yeah, but I'm the new guy. The wild card. If someone's been killing your patients, then they couldn't have expected that Dixon would find the radioactive stash, or that Gabney would fire him to keep the gossip from impacting the awards. They couldn't have expected that I'd actually do my job and figure out Ida Mae's body was hot."

She drew away from him, shaking her head. "No. I can't believe it. I won't. Someone has been killing my patients? Nuking them? It makes no sense."

But it did, in a horribly simple way, and they both knew it. Cage asked, "Would you prefer to believe that your own treatments killed five women and left their bodies radioactive?"

She shook her head, tucked her chin against her chest and murmured, "No. I didn't. I couldn't."

He nodded, though part of him knew it would be easier, safer to think her at fault. But that part was smaller now, and the greater part of him held out his arms to the pale, shaky woman who had captivated him from the first moment their eyes had locked. "Then we'll figure it out together. Come here."

"I can't." She backed away a pace. "I can't be…"

"Weak," he finished for her, remembering that she'd said that before, right after he'd pulled her out of the closet, thinking her dead. "I won't tell anyone. I promise." Though he wondered who had taught her that lesson.

The father she'd mentioned? Or someone else?

The flash of jealousy brought a quick memory of his wife's blond hair and her pale blue eyes. And then Ripley was in his arms, her compact body smaller and curvier than Heather's had been. And alive. So alive.

Then their lips touched almost without conscious decision, and for the first time in five long years, Cage felt something other than anger. Guilt. Numbness.

Suddenly, he could feel it all again. Heat. Electricity. Passion. In the first instant, he thought that he'd find none of his wife's sweetness in Ripley Davis. And in the next instant he couldn't think at all.

He dove into her mouth, into the wild, wanton vortex of energy that suddenly crackled around them, born partly from fear, partly from need. She tasted of dark, forbidden pleasures and wild passion. He felt the power rise in him, a power he'd only ever felt before when the crowds screamed his name and his fingers found the baseball's familiar seams.

Crushing her closer, he explored the dark reaches of her mouth with his tongue, wanting to be closer to that exotic, seductive power. Wanting to be closer to her. Wanting to turn the clock back to the time when he was that cocky young pitcher with a wife at home and his whole life ahead of him.

When Ripley pushed away and took two big steps back, it was as if she'd yanked all of it away from him again. He felt the pressure in his chest and reached for her.

"Cage, this isn't a good—" The pager at her belt sounded, and Cage dimly realized it wasn't the first of the annoying beeps. She tried again. "I didn't mean—" She checked the display and her lips flattened to a thin line. "I have to go."

The taste of her still rocketed through his system, setting off every *Warning!* buzzer he possessed. He should stay far away from Ripley. She was dangerous to his equilibrium. His purpose. But he shook his head, knowing he had to stay close to her. Had to protect her. "*We'll* go. I'm not letting you out of my sight unless I'm sure you're safe."

Her eyes searched his for a moment, then she nodded.

"Okay." She glanced around the room and her eyes locked on the contaminated slides. She touched a finger to her lower lip, which was swollen from his kisses. Then she glanced down at the beeper display, which Cage saw read simply *Milo*.

He thought of the fragile child and his stomach clenched at the realization that the boy, like the rest of her patients, could be in danger.

They stared at each other for a long moment before she turned for the door, called to the side of a small, sick boy. Her words were muffled, reluctant. Afraid. "If I'm in danger, then so are you, Cage. You're involved in this investigation just as much as I am. You need to watch your back."

He draped an arm across her shoulders, noticing again how much smaller she was than Heather had been. *Fragile,* said his mind again. *Vulnerable.*

"We'll watch each other's backs," he said quietly when they reached the elevators. "Partners, okay?"

She stared at him a beat before finally nodding. "Okay." She stuck out a hand and they shook on it. "Partners."

Neither of them commented on the electricity that arced at the contact. Or on the eyes they felt watching from the shadows as they climbed into the elevator. But like the chemistry between them, the feeling of being watched was present.

And powerful.

Chapter Six

When they entered the Oncology patient area, Cage stood aside as Ripley slipped into Milo's room. His heartbeat leveled to see the child propped up in bed, weak but alive. The page hadn't been another R-ONC death.

Five patients dead of heart failure, he thought. Radioactively contaminated. *Hospital killer. Serial killer.* The words rippled from half-forgotten headlines, taunting him when he acknowledged that he and Ripley still had no hard evidence.

As Gabney had pointed out, the threats to Ripley's life could be unrelated, accidental. The bodies could have been contaminated during a faulty treatment.

They had no evidence of a killer, though Cage believed in his gut that they were dealing with one. He just hoped to God they could gather enough evidence to stop it before the person struck again.

Before another patient died. Or a doctor.

"Belle. Why are you still here? What's Milo's status and where's Dr. Campbell?" Ripley fired questions at a tiny woman in a volunteer's uniform. Cage vaguely remembered having seen her pushing the boy's wheelchair earlier that day.

"I'm here because he needed me, Dr. Davis. The good Lord knows his parents don't make much time for the little tyke." Belle's lips thinned to a line. "He's having a bad night. One of the nurses mentioned seeing you in the elevator, so I took it upon myself to see if you have a minute to sit with him."

Ripley nodded as though it was perfectly reasonable to be paged to a child's bedside at midnight on a Friday. But he saw her shoulders relax. She blew out a breath. "Of course." She glanced at Cage. "I'll be fine, there are plenty of people around, even this late at night. Why don't you go home and get some sleep?"

He stood in the doorway of the little boy's room, not quite ready to leave, but unable to step through the door.

Belle touched his sleeve. "You can go in if you want."

Cage shook his head. "I'll stay out here." The chemical smells surrounded him with memory, and in Ripley's eyes he saw a gentle compassion he didn't associate with doctors. The little boy's lips moved and she nodded in response. Cage stepped back. "What about his parents?" he asked through a throat that had suddenly grown tight.

Belle tightened her lips. "They think it's enough that their insurance pays for the treatments, but it's not. Lord knows, it's the time spent that counts. He needs their help. Their love."

Cage took another step away, but the details of the little room wouldn't leave. The cheerful red, white and blue of the Boston pennants stuck above Milo's bed were a stark contrast to the child's thin, pale face. Cage saw a baseball bat lying beside the boy's stick-thin arm, and his stomach clenched at the dreams so obviously displayed. So clearly unrealistic.

His imagination tried to superimpose the image of a long, lithe blond woman, but failed. He'd never visited Heather in the hospital.

He'd been on the road.

"He likes baseball?" Cage closed his eyes against the guilt that slammed through him, fresher now than the numb feelings he'd been chasing for the five years since her death. He tasted Ripley on his lips and thought of his wife.

"Loves it," Belle answered simply. "He wants to be a pitcher when he grows up."

Neither of them voiced the obvious, that the child would be lucky to grow up. Cage shook his head and turned for the outer door. He had to get away from the hospital for a while, away from the sights and the smells. Ripley was right, she'd be safe in the well-lit, well-populated patients' wing. And he needed some air. "Tell Dr. Davis I'll meet her back here in an hour."

In his office, Cage scanned his clothing for trace radioactivity, as he always did before leaving the job, just in case he'd come in contact with slight contamination at one of the nuke-using labs. He frowned at a small hot spot on his sleeve, then stripped the shirt off and tossed it in the "wait a bit" basket where they stored their contaminated clothing until the counts faded. He pulled on a spare shirt as he strode down the deserted corridor and pushed through the revolving doors into the deep Chinatown night.

His wife's ghost seemed to keep pace with him as he

drove to the penthouse they'd once shared. The memory didn't nag or berate him. Not Heather. It wasn't her way.

No, the blond wisp seemed to touch his cheek and whisper, *It's okay. I understand.* And that was somehow worse. Her memory forgave him for kissing another woman now just as readily as she'd forgiven him for being away so often when she'd been alive.

But Cage would never forgive himself. He'd been lousy as a husband and worse as a man. His work at Boston General was just the beginning. He had no family, no ties. He could keep moving indefinitely from hospital to hospital, seeking out doctors who cared more for profit and career than for their patients.

He could bring them down and protect other women. Other wives. Because, damn it, doctors were all the same.

Except Ripley, whispered his mind. *She cares for her patients. She's not like the others.*

But part of him still wasn't sure about that. Even after their kiss, he still doubted. What if she was playing him? He couldn't trust that she was everything she seemed.

Because if she was real, she was a woman he thought he could care about. It would be better for him, and for her, if that never happened.

"Good evening, Mr. Cage." The doorman tipped his hat as Cage entered the building he'd bought with his signing bonus. The rental income together with his former seven-figure salary had made him a rich man.

But not rich enough to save his wife. Or to avenge her death.

Cage nodded. "Charlie."

The elevator ride to the top floor seemed to take longer

than ever, as though home was farther away each time he tried to get there.

In the foyer, the double doors of the big closet loomed large and Cage hesitated a moment before opening them for the first time in so many years. It was all there. The boxes the ball club had shipped back after he quit. The things he'd packed away the day he'd stripped Heather's room back to the walls, hoping to ease the pain.

And the canvas bag he'd tossed aside when he came into the condo the last night she'd been alive.

He rubbed a hand across his heart, sat on the floor, and reached for the bag. There was something he needed to do, then he would head back to Boston General to sit with Ripley.

To protect her. To watch her, though he wasn't sure anymore exactly what he was watching for.

THE BUSTLE OF THE changing nurses' shift woke Ripley near 6:00 a.m., and she groaned at the familiar aches and pains that came with sleeping at a patient's bedside. Milo stirred, and the tug at the back of her throat reminded Ripley of her dream. Hissing chemicals. The stink of chlorine gas. Fear.

Then she remembered the rest. She muffled a groan and rested her head near the little boy's leg.

Ida Mae. Four other patients dead and contaminated. Mr. Harris and the closet. Danger. And Cage, who was another sort of danger. She touched a finger to her lips, where the imprint of their kiss still lingered. He had tasted of dark need and grief, an unexpected flare of power mixed with sweetness. His taste, and his kiss, had been complicated. Like Cage himself. Like the situation.

Ripley shivered and she touched Milo's hand where it wrapped around his beloved baseball bat. She had to keep her patients safe. *Had to.* If anything happened to Milo, or to the others, she would never forgive herself. Thinking of the others, she stood and slowly crossed the room to look in on the woman across the hall in the adult oncology unit.

Janice Cooper slept peacefully, with a soft half smile on her face. Her treatments were going well, Ripley knew. With luck, the new grandmother would be released in a few days. Perhaps even before she finished crocheting the baby sweater she worked on a little each day.

"Dr. Davis? Everything okay in here?" The quick jolt of fear at the unexpected voice was short-lived, fading when Ripley realized it was only Belle.

"What are you still doing here?"

The volunteer smiled gently. "I went home several hours ago and caught a few winks. Now I'm back, ready for the new day. At my age, you don't need much sleep, you know?"

Not for the first time, Ripley wondered exactly how old Belle was. She could be anywhere from forty to sixty. She always wore conservative, high-necked dresses and flat-soled shoes that made almost no noise when she walked. It added to her air of serenity.

Serenity. Peace. That was something Ripley sorely needed right now. She glanced back at Milo and was relieved to see some color in his face. Maybe he'd make it through this round of treatments, after all.

She stood and touched Belle's sleeve in passing. "If you see Mr. Cage, let him know I've gone to the chapel, okay?"

She was surprised he wasn't dozing in the reception area, waiting for her. And a little disappointed, which wasn't fair. She'd told him to go home. Told him she'd be safe in Oncology. But a small, scared, un-Davislike part of her would have liked him at her side as she headed for the doctors' lounge near her office. Feeling every one of her thirty-two years in the creak of her joints and the soreness in her throat and neck, Ripley showered and changed into a fresh shirt and yesterday's jeans, looking over her shoulder all the while. Her mind raced and she found herself jumping at the shadows behind the locker doors, at the billow of a hospital-issue shower curtain.

At the echoing quiet of the lounge.

She quickly dried her hair and escaped back into the hallway, trying to laugh her nerves away and failing. With her mind on finding someplace peaceful, someplace safe, she headed for the hospital chapel, one floor down from R-ONC.

In the hallway outside the chapel, Ripley was startled to see one of the Radiation Safety techs coming toward her. He nodded in greeting, "Dr. Davis."

"Whistler. What are you doing here? Has Cage instituted weekend shifts?" She couldn't help the quick flash of nerves, though the young man had never worried her before.

He grinned. "No, ma'am. A few of us met here last night to go out dancing and my girlfriend left her jacket in the office. I'm just earning points by getting it for her." He lifted the faded denim coat and Ripley nodded, relaxing. He was just at the hospital to pick up a coat. Nothing sinister.

Still, she was suddenly anxious to escape into the small chapel. It represented sanctuary. Safety. After all, who would violate a church?

Her smile felt forced. "Well then, I won't hold you up. Have a nice weekend." She sketched a wave and slipped inside the chapel.

Instantly, she was surrounded by peace and the smell of fresh flowers. The chapel was dark, but she didn't bother to flick on the lights near the door. The fat candle near the altar illuminated the space well enough, and she welcomed the privacy darkness provided. She slid onto a bench and let her mind settle as the warm shadows embraced her. Safe. She was safe here.

Though she'd not been raised in any particular faith, Ripley visited the dark, scented room when she was worried about a patient, or about herself. The silence helped her clear her mind for a few minutes, and the elegantly carved crucifix at the front of the narrow room let her believe someone was actually listening to her prayers.

Let her believe someone cared.

But not today. There was no peace for Ripley, not even in the small chapel. Her mind churned with thoughts and worries. Milo. Her other patients. Herself. Her department.

Cage.

In those last few moments before he'd kissed her, she'd seen the intent in his black eyes. She'd known it was a mistake, known she should have backed away. But instead, she'd leaned forward and accepted his kiss. Returned it. And in the instant that her arms had slid around his neck, she'd known there would be trouble between them. The attraction was too strong, the taste of him too compelling. And there were too many reasons why they would never work together. He was too driven, too moody. Too strong a personality.

He was exactly the sort of man she'd sworn to avoid.

"What am I doing?" she whispered into the echoing darkness, feeling the shadows creep closer.

A sly shift of sound was returned to her, and the hairs on the back of her neck stood up. It could have been an echo.

Or it could have been a stealthy, quiet footstep.

"Hello?" she called, standing up and feeling her heart rattle in her chest. "Is someone there?"

Nobody answered. Ripley peered into the heavily shadowed alcoves, straining her eyes when she thought she caught a slide of motion in the darkness beside the stained glass. "Hello?" Her injured voice cracked on the word.

Then the candle winked out. The chapel was plunged into sudden, complete darkness.

And Ripley could hear someone else breathing.

IT WAS CLOSE TO SIX-FIFTEEN Saturday morning when Cage charged up the hospital steps. He couldn't believe he'd fallen asleep on the closet floor. He only hoped Ripley had been sensible enough to stay in the patients' wing where there were plenty of people around. But when he reached Oncology, he found Milo alone and awake.

"Livvy remembered where she'd seen you before," the boy said in his breathy voice. "You used to pitch for Texas."

The reminder was a poignant counterpart to the memories Cage had discovered in the hallway closet. He nodded, and felt his heart ache beneath the layers of scar tissue. "Yeah. I used to pitch for Texas." But the fears of the present were stronger than the regrets of the past, and he quickly asked, "Do you know where Dr. Rip went?"

"I heard her tell Belle she was going to the chapel, I think. I was most of the way asleep." Milo replied, his voice rasping with the effort it cost him to talk.

The chapel? That seemed like an un-Ripleyish place to go. But then again, how well did he really know her?

He knew how she tasted, he thought, and cursed the rev of his body at the reminder. The chemistry between them was an unforeseen complication. An impossible one that filled his brain with useless wishes, much as the memories did.

Then he thought of the chapel, small and isolated off a main corridor downstairs, and a quick chill dispelled both arousal and confusion. Why the hell had she gone down there? She had promised to stay safe, damn it!

Milo interrupted his thoughts. "Will you come to the game with us this week? I'm sure Ripley won't mind. The Tammy Fund has a box right over the Boston dugout..." He trailed off to breathe and Cage shook his head.

"Sorry." He handed Milo his old pitcher's mitt, rescued from the bottom of his team duffel. "But I brought you this. I don't need it anymore."

He was out the door before the boy found breath to thank him, which was just fine with Cage. He didn't want thanks. He just wanted to leave the memories behind. Again. He wasn't sure what had compelled him to go home and get the glove, but he hadn't questioned the impulse.

It had felt important. Almost as important as finding Ripley now and making sure she was safe.

He jogged down the stairs, trying to convince himself everything was fine even though the hairs on the back of his neck were standing at attention. Then he turned the corner to the chapel.

And heard her scream.

"Ripley!" He charged the rest of the way to the door and kicked it open.

The chapel was completely dark. The smell of flowers was cloying. Overpowering. He heard a scuffling noise and slapped for the light switch just inside the door. "Ripley?"

"Cage!" She bolted up the aisle and clung to him. He could feel her heart pounding as he held her tight, shielding her with his body while he searched the small room for her attacker.

The chapel was deserted.

"Ripley, what's wrong? What happened?" He tried to push her away so he could check for injuries, but she burrowed into him so tightly it was impossible. "Are you hurt?"

Her voice was muffled against his chest. "No, I'm okay. I'm not hurt." The arms around his waist loosened and Cage's panic level subsided. In its place, a new heat bloomed, centered on the place where her high, firm breasts pressed against his chest and her hips aligned with his.

How long had it been since he'd simply held a woman?

As quickly as the thought came, the answer charged on its heels. It had been five years since Heather had died in his arms. He would not allow such a thing to happen again.

If it did, it would happen over his dead body.

The heat fled and Cage set Ripley away. "What happened? Why was it so dark in here?"

He saw her struggle to master her breathing. Saw the dull red flush that climbed her cheeks. She gestured. "The candle was lit, but then it went out. I thought I heard someone in here with me and I panicked."

Cage prowled the chapel, but found nothing. No evidence. There was a small door behind a stained-glass panel, but it was firmly locked. "There's nobody here now." But even as he said it, he remembered the broom closet key in his pocket. Locks were made to be opened. "What exactly happened? And why the hell didn't you stay in the patients' wing?" he demanded with sudden ferocity, anger following the rush of relief.

"Don't shout at me!" she snapped, "Nothing happened, okay? There was nobody here, you can see for yourself. I panicked. I was weak and hysterical and I talked myself into believing there was someone here when there wasn't. And you're right. I should have stayed with Milo. I was wrong and you were right. Are you satisfied?"

He was nowhere close to satisfied, but he saw by the hint of wildness in her eyes and the subtle tremor of her hands that she needed more from him than a lecture. And perhaps he needed it, too. So he folded her into his arms and rested his cheek in her hair and simply said, "I'm sorry. It scared the hell out of me when I heard you scream."

And just like that, the fight went out of her. She sagged against him and wrapped her arms around his waist as though he was the last thing keeping her upright. The heat built between them, but it was different this time, a binding warmth rather than a crackling blaze. He heard her murmur, "I scared the hell out of me, too." She sounded ashamed.

"Don't worry. I won't tell anyone." He released her and held out a hand. "Come on, I'll buy you a cup of coffee. I think we need a plan."

Outside the café, Ripley turned to speak to Cage and got a nasty shock when she recognized the man approaching from the other direction.

Howard Davis. Her father. She stiffened her spine and lifted her chin, unconsciously stepping between him and Cage, hoping to prevent a confrontation.

But with Howard, there was almost always a confrontation.

"Caroline." He stopped a few feet away and made no move to hug her, or even shake her hand. He raked his gaze down her slept-in jeans and spare shirt. "You're a mess!"

For a brief moment, she would've given anything to be able to throw herself into her father's arms and bawl like a baby. There were too many things on her shoulders right now, too many fears and pressures.

But that would be showing emotion. And like weakness, Davises didn't show emotion in public.

"Caroline?" The word cracked like a whip, but Ripley

refused to flinch at her father's tone. Cage stood at her shoulder. She felt the warmth of his arm barely grazing hers and thought maybe she could lean on him a bit, just for now.

"And you are?" Cage's question was soft, but the steel beneath the words was unmistakable.

"On my way to Leo Gabney's office to straighten out the mess you've gotten yourself into." Howard ignored Cage and spoke to his daughter, bringing the full weight of paternal disapproval to bear.

"You'll do nothing of the sort, Father," she snapped, aware that her resentment from last night's phone call was still simmering along with the other complications she'd fallen into. Cage. Leo. Ida Mae. *Danger.* "I told you last night to stay out of this and I meant it."

It was sad that she didn't trust her father enough to tell him that her life was in danger. How hurtful that she didn't trust him to take her side. But then, Boston General had always been more important to Howard Davis than his family.

He took a deep breath. "Caroline, I don't think—"

"Excuse me, but Dr. Davis prefers to be called Ripley."

There was dead silence for a heartbeat after Cage's pronouncement, and she felt a spurt of gratitude even as she braced herself for the explosion. It had been a long time since anyone had sided with her against her father.

"And you would be *Mr.* Cage, correct?" Howard emphasized the "mister" as though non-doctors were beneath his notice.

"That's right. I'm the new RSO. And you are?" The men traded glare for glare.

"Dr. Howard Davis, Head Administrator emeritus and

current head of the Board of Directors," Ripley's father answered with a superior smirk. "I know very well who you are, Mr. Cage. I know all about you." The smirk widened, making it clear that the things Howard knew were not particularly nice.

Cage surged forward a half step and Ripley put her hand on his sleeve as though her touch could hold him back.

Surprisingly, it did. He stopped and looked down at the place where her hand lingered. So did Howard. His lip curled. "So that's where this attitude of yours is coming from, Caroline. You've fallen for the new bad boy." He snorted. "You do things like this to embarrass me, don't you?"

Ripley snapped, "No, Father. That's just a bonus. And our relationship—or lack thereof—is none of your business."

Howard's smile was icy. Displeased. "Grow up, Caroline, and understand how your actions reflect upon your mother and I." He took a step back, though Ripley knew he was far from retreating.

She sighed. "You and Mother haven't shared the same house in years, Father, and I'm not sure why you keep up the pretense of speaking for her. Besides, Mother could care less who I'm seeing as long as I'm happy."

"And how long will that be, Caroline? Until he leaves you alone to die while he attends a fancy dinner party? That's what happened to his first wife, you know."

Sick distress rattled through Ripley. It wasn't surprise, particularly, as she'd known the shadows of guilt and grief in Cage's eyes had to come from a woman. It was pain that she'd learned of it from her own father.

"You *bastard*. Don't you *dare* speak of her!" Cage's voice cracked with the force of his growl.

"Father!" she snapped, hating the little hospital spies, who never reported anything good. Hating her father. Hurting for Cage. "I think you'd better leave."

"Caroline—"

"And for God's sake call me Ripley!"

Clearly wishing he was having this conversation on the phone so he could hang up, Howard Davis tugged stiffly at his cuffs and retreated. "I see that we'll have to continue this when you're feeling more reasonable, Caroline. I'll be in touch." He turned and left without a backward glance.

Ripley watched him go with the same old wish in her heart. *I wish that things were different. I wish that* he *were different*. But wishing had never made it so before and it wasn't likely to start now.

She took a deep, hurting breath, and glanced at Cage. His eyes were dark and angry, his jaw set. "Cage, I'm sorry. I—"

He cut her off with a gesture. "I'd rather not talk about it. Let's get our coffee and head back to R-ONC. I think we should start by scanning that whole area for nukes." He strode into the café, leaving her standing in the hall.

Alone.

Chapter Seven

That's what happened to his first wife. Howard Davis's words rattled around in Cage's brain as he slid the Geiger counter across the last box of saline bags. But he barely saw the neat row of injectable supplies they were scanning for contamination. He saw only the disdain in the face of Ripley's father.

The horror in hers.

It hadn't surprised him that the administrators knew of his part in Heather's death. What surprised him was the shame he'd felt at not having been the one to tell Ripley. She'd had to hear it from her father, a man who wouldn't even call her by her right name.

The hurt in her face had warned him more eloquently than words that he needed to protect her from more than the menace at Boston General. He would also have to protect her from the thing that was growing between them.

And protect himself, as well.

"Well, there's nothing here." Ripley gave a last swing of the Geiger counter and shook her head. "Though negative data is still data, I suppose." She braced both hands on her lower back and stretched out the kinks. The material of her shirt pulled tight across her high, firm breasts.

Her words echoed in the storage room, the first either of them had spoken since she had offered a tentative apology for her father's behavior and Cage had snarled her to silence.

"Yeah," he agreed in a voice that felt rusty. Unused. "None of this stuff is hot."

Unfortunately, the boxes of injectables were about the only things in the room that weren't hot. The thermostat in the little storeroom must be set at a hundred. Cage tugged at his collar and gritted his teeth. That was the reason his body temperature was roaring out of control. It had nothing to do with the way Ripley's jeans fit across her tight rear, or the single dark curl that had escaped the sleek ponytail she'd fashioned before they began searching for radioactively contaminated stocks.

Off-limits, he told himself. *You're going to protect her until the two of you can find evidence that will force Gabney to call in the authorities. Then you'll get the hell out of her life before you're responsible for hurting two women rather than just one.*

"Let's check the broom closet next." Only the faintest whisper of hesitation in her voice betrayed Ripley's reluctance to go there.

"I'll be right behind you," he said, "and remember, I've got the key. Besides, we don't have many other options until I can reach George Dixon and see what he remembers about finding those nukes." He draped an arm across her shoulder and steered her out of the storeroom.

Then he dropped his arm, remembering her father.

Remembering that she deserved better than a man who had already failed one woman he'd sworn to protect.

Heather. The pain ripped as it had five years ago, though dulled some by time. He could clearly picture the granite marker with her name carved above a simple Christian sentiment. But her exact image had grown blurry, static, as though it was a photograph that had faded with time. The thought that he was finally losing her brought an ache to Cage's chest.

And made him long to reach for Ripley. Made him yearn to save her as he hadn't saved his wife.

He was tired, Cage decided when a dull throb began behind his eyes. The stress of the past few days was catching up with him. That was why he was overwhelmed by the desire to turn off the lights in the supply room, sit against the back wall, and draw her down beside him. It was the only reason he wanted to hold her hand and tell her about his wife.

"Cage?" She touched his arm and he flinched as the contact sparked something primitive and needy deep inside.

"I'm fine," he said curtly, though she hadn't asked. "It's nothing. Let's get out of here."

He slapped the lights off on his way out the door and ignored the beckoning warm darkness, but the itchy, twitchy sensation didn't fade as they walked side by side to the broom closet near R-ONC. Cage stared at the letters on the department door, trying to summon the memory of Heather's wasted, burned body. But in his mind's eye her golden hair blurred to dark, and her pale skin glowed with a tan of sun and health until he wasn't picturing Heather at all.

"Damn it!" He opened the broom closet so hard the door rattled against a rack of mops and brushes and sprang back at him. Ripley jumped, clearly nervous, but saved her worry for him.

"Cage?" She touched his arm, and he spun toward her, baring his teeth and fighting the urge to take what hadn't been offered. She asked, "Are you okay?" When he didn't answer right away, she looked down. "I really am sorry, you know, for what my father said. He had no right. I know you don't want to talk about it, but I wanted to say that I'm sorry about your wife. You must have loved her very much."

If only he had. If only he'd been a better husband. He might still have a family. He might still be that boy in the baseball cap.

The pressure behind his eyes intensified, and he clenched his jaw against the need to howl. Where were all these memories coming from? Why now? He'd laid his wife to rest a long time ago. He'd moved on with his life.

Hadn't he?

"Cage?" Maybe it was the instincts of a healer, maybe the instincts of a woman, but Ripley's eyes searched his, dark and concerned. "Cage, talk to me." The hand on his arm slid up and touched his cheek.

The pain behind his eyes sharpened, and his vision blurred with unfamiliar wetness. He heard the clatter of heels approaching from an intersecting hallway and forestalled the obligatory "Hi, how are you?" exchange by yanking Ripley into the broom closet and shutting the door over her faint protest.

It was a mistake. He knew it the moment the latch clicked and his body bumped up against hers in the darkness. She gasped slightly at the contact and his heart thundered in his ears.

He fumbled for the dangling cord of the single light bulb and was only vaguely surprised when he pulled it and nothing happened. The footsteps passed in the hallway before fading again, but neither of them moved to open the door. Cage closed his eyes and felt the headache recede as a new tension took over.

Over the taint of chlorine, he could smell the lingering fragrance of her shampoo and a hint of the chocolate bar he knew she'd smuggled to Milo. And in the tiny, awkward broom closet where Ripley had almost died the day before, the realization hit Cage like a fist to the chest. She wasn't anything like the doctors he'd known. She cared. She felt her patients' pain. She hurt when they hurt. She understood. And it was that understanding that opened the barriers around his heart, just a crack.

"I was a lousy husband," he said into the darkness, and it helped knowing she was there, listening. "I was on the road all the time, never at home with her where I belonged. We used to talk about the things we'd do when I was finished pitching for Texas. Five years, maybe eight if I got lucky and my shoulder held out, then we were going to be together like a normal married couple." *Have a baby,* whispered a quiet voice in the back of his mind, making his soul ache.

He let his head drop forward, and found that his brow rested perfectly on the top of Ripley's head. And though it was so wrong, it felt *right.* He let out a big sigh and their breaths mingled in warm intimacy.

She drew back slightly. "My father was like that when I was growing up. By the time he left Boston General, my mother had packed her bags. She got tired of waiting around for him to come home for dinner, so when I left for med school, she escaped for the fairways."

Oddly, the comparison angered Cage. Though he scourged himself often enough over neglecting Heather, he didn't like that Ripley saw parallels between him and Howard Davis. He reached for her, holding her still when she would have drawn away. "I'm not your father, Ripley."

"And I'm not your wife," she fired back, "but I can feel you comparing us whenever I get too close to you. Long before my father said anything, I knew she was there in your mind. And even if I wanted something serious to happen between us, I'd know it was no use—because no living woman will ever match up to her."

Cage bowed his head, knowing she was right about one thing, but not the other. It was true that he'd compared her to Heather time and again. But it wasn't Ripley he'd found lacking. "Ripley, I—"

"It doesn't matter, Cage," she told him gently, moving to stand closer, just a breath away. "Because I'm not looking for something serious between us. I don't do serious, it's just not worth it." She touched his face, and her fingertips left flames behind.

The darkness pressed them together. Footsteps in the hallway approached, then paused. Feeling a frisson of fear ripple through her, Cage leaned down until her warmth feathered his face. "Don't worry, I'll keep you safe."

It wasn't until another set of footsteps met the first in the hallway, and cheerful female voices rose in greeting, that he realized just how close he and Ripley had gotten to each other. Just a breath away. And when both women moved off down the corridor together, he leaned down, or she leaned up, he couldn't say which. He just knew that one moment they were two separate people, and the next they were joined as their lips met and clung.

And the fire ignited.

It was the same as it had been before only more so. Cage almost staggered with the impact when Ripley wrapped her arms around his neck and kissed him as if her very life depended on it. And then it was *his* life in the balance, as the breath backed up in his lungs and his heart stuttered with the feel of her in his arms.

He'd expected the power this time, expected the bittersweet nostalgia of a cocky young man who'd lost everything. Heather was so close to the surface of his mind right then. It was so dark in the little closet. If he'd wanted to, he could have pretended it was her gasp he swallowed, her hand that guided his to touch a breast through thin, clinging fabric.

Her nipple that pointed in his palm.

But the larger part of him knew it was Ripley's taste that exploded on his tongue and Ripley's fingers that dug into his shoulders as he deepened the kiss and wedged his leg between hers, needing to get closer to her warmth. Closer.

He'd been cold for so very, very long.

He tore his mouth free long enough to ask, "Are you sure?"

"I'm tired of being afraid, Cage. I'm tired of looking over my shoulder and thinking that everyone I meet in the hall could be a killer. I need this, right here, right now," she said between kisses as her busy fingers unbuttoned most of his shirt and she transferred her mouth to his chest. "I need to feel alive. I need to feel like there's something beyond the hospital. Can't you feel it?"

And the hell of it was, he *could* feel it. He felt the press of reality beyond the broom-closet door. He felt the security of the small, dark space, and the knowledge that once he pulled the key from his pocket and slipped it into the lock on their side, nobody could unlock it from the outside. From the reality side.

"I feel it," he said, and kissed her again. Fast. It was all happening so fast against a backdrop of breathing and sighs, rustling cloth and frantic whispers. The walls seemed to press close. Cage felt a row of shelves at his back and was grateful for the support when his knees threatened to buckle. Remembering the bottles of cleaning fluid, he shoved away from the shelving and spun them around, banging his bad shoulder against the door in an effort to find support. "But Ripley, I can't promise you anything."

"I don't want promises, Cage. Promises are what my father gave my mother. I don't want them. I just want not to be alone right now. I just want you to be with me." He wasn't even sure she knew what she was saying anymore, as her busy mouth traveled down his stomach and his fingers tangled in her hair. He flung his other arm backward, flailing for an anchor amidst the whirling sensations. He didn't think his legs were going to hold him much longer. All the blood in his body seemed suddenly concentrated elsewhere.

He leaned back, hard, against the door and boosted her up to wrap her legs around his waist. Then they were perfectly aligned, mouth to mouth. Center to center. Need to need.

Where had all this feeling come from? The warmth swamped him. The greed almost flattened him. And the hot, groping want roared up and battered down some of the cold emptiness that had been with him, it seemed, forever.

Oh, yes. He knew about being alone.

His hands slid up her torso to touch her breasts beneath a sly slide of lace. He could feel the softest place, where the smooth skin gave way to crinkled flesh and hard points. She arched against him as his mouth found one of those tight little buds through her shirt.

The room spun. Faster. Harder. Her legs loosened at his waist and she dropped her feet to the floor. Cage felt his zipper give way. When she freed him, the smooth slide of her hand had his head snapping back. Five years worth of needs, maybe even a lifetime's worth, was suddenly centered on a single point of contact.

If he didn't have her, then and there, he might die. But there were practicalities he couldn't avoid.

"Wait. I...I haven't got..." This was a hospital, he thought with insane clarity. There had to be a condom somewhere. Anywhere.

"Don't worry about it, this is for both of us" she said,

and he burrowed his fingers in her hair as she kissed his lips one last time, then trailed her way down his chest, and lower…

His fingers tightened and he spread his legs to brace himself. "Don't. You don't have to if you don't want to—"

Apparently she did want to. He swore sharply, reverently, when her lips closed over him in one sure, bold move. His buttocks clenched as every molecule of his body concentrated itself in one hard, pulsing place. He clenched his teeth to keep from yelling when her clever mouth and silky tongue took another deadly swing at the barriers around his soul.

He dug his fingers into her scalp, into her shoulders as he felt the power build. He felt cherished. Healed. Wanted.

Needed. And that was the most dangerous feeling of all.

Pulling her up, he somehow got her jeans down to her knees. Her hand found his slick shaft and her mouth fused to his as Cage held her off the ground with one arm and stroked his other hand straight down her stomach to the wet, waiting, wanting place below.

Though his fingers found her center with more force than finesse, she stiffened against him and whimpered into his mouth, "Cage."

"Yeah, honey." Almost beyond himself from the friction of her hand, he found the hard little button within its velvet folds and stroked it once, twice. She turned her head into his shirt and tried to muffle a scream as her body jerked and he felt the hard pulses begin. Her hand tightened, and when he poured himself into her palm, the pleasure carried a knife-edge of pain, as though he'd lost a part of himself in the spasm.

And then he didn't care. He didn't care that he was half propped up against the door of a stinking broom closet. He didn't care that his pants were around his ankles or that she'd never unbuttoned the collar of his shirt.

He cared only for the woman wrapped around him, still shaking with the last precious aftershocks. Their scent surrounded him. Filled him.

Humbled him and gloried him.

How long had it been since he'd felt this relaxed, this complete? A ghost's whisper at the back of his mind knew the answer, but he chose to ignore it. This wasn't about the past. It was about right now.

He turned his lips into her hair and cuddled her against his chest, trusting his legs to hold out another minute. When she murmured and snuggled close, he smiled and rested his cheek on her head, knowing something fundamental had happened between them. Within him. And when she whispered, "Cage," in a wondering murmur that told him he wasn't alone, he smiled and whispered her name.

The suddenness with which she pushed off his chest was no more startling than the open hand that cracked across his cheek.

"What the hell?" He jolted away from the door and stumbled, feeling his pants cling at his ankles. "What's wrong? I thought—"

"Well, you thought wrong," she spat, adding as an afterthought, "Jerk." She yanked her jeans up before she opened the door, then she jammed her shirt into the waist-band and glared at him in the half light. "I'm going to say this one more time, okay?" He winced as the volume increased. *"My name is Ripley!"*

And she was gone, leaving the door half open and Cage standing bare-assed in the center of the broom closet. He groaned, then swore aloud when he realized that he'd just done the unthinkable.

He'd called her Heather.

MOVING FAST UNDER A cloud of righteous indignation, Ripley rounded the corner just outside her office and ran headfirst into Cage's assistant, Whistler. And as quickly as that, fear replaced the anger. How had she forgotten, even for a moment, what was happening in her department?

"What are you doing here?" she barked, part of her fearing there had been another emergency call, and part of her registering that though Whistler had no official business at Boston General on the weekend, she'd seen him twice now.

The radiation tech blinked. "Picking up some log-books I forgot on Friday?"

"Are you asking me or telling me?" she snapped with a blend of nerves and hurt, then winced because it sounded like something her father would say. "Sorry, I'm in a filthy mood."

"That's okay." Whistler shrugged. "I'm not big on working weekends, either."

Yet he'd been at the hospital both days. A shiver tickled at the base of her spine. "Why is that, exactly?"

Whistler glanced at the green loose-leaf binders tucked in the crook of his left arm. "Because of the new boss. And the radioactive bodies. Take your pick." Before she could respond, he glanced down the hall behind her. "Speaking of which, have you seen Cage? His coat is in the office, but I can't find him."

The name sent a bolt through Ripley that was equal parts lust, anger and guilt. She wouldn't forgive his calling her the wrong name. But she was a grown woman. She knew seducing a man with baggage was a sure road to disaster.

Lucky for her, she had her emotions securely strapped in for the ride. She muttered, "We were scanning the injectables for contamination."

One of the binders fell to the floor with a clatter. Muttering an apology, Whistler fumbled to retrieve it, almost losing the others in the process. When he straightened, he edged around her. "You know where he is now?"

"In the broom closet," she said, feeling a vague disquiet, and a sense of guilt when the radiation tech muttered a goodbye and bolted for the closet. Then she remembered being cradled in Cage's strong arms while his heart beat a steady, sated rhythm beneath her cheek. She remembered thinking that maybe *this* was what the poets got so excited about, the thing that bound two people together close enough that they would gladly die to save each other.

She remembered thinking that maybe *this* was what led to happily ever after.

Then she remembered hearing him whisper his dead wife's name and she didn't feel mean anymore. She felt justified. And as she grabbed her coat from her office, she found herself hoping that Cage still had his pants down when Whistler opened the door.

RIPLEY'S APARTMENT seemed so empty without a Siamese yowling at the door that she almost climbed the stairs right away to retrieve Simon. Then she remembered it was bingo night for most of her neighbors. The cat-sitter wouldn't be home until well after ten.

The blinking answering machine provided the only motion in the simple living room, and butterflies chased each other around in her stomach as she punched the play button.

What if there was nobody on the other end of the line?

The machine beeped and a scratchy, tinny version of Tansy's voice filled the room. "Rip? I wanted to let you know that I'll be in late tomorrow. I have…something I need to do. Okay? So I'll see you around lunchtime." Tansy's voice seemed odd, and she paused a moment before hanging up. A dull dread settled in Ripley's chest and she was across the room, picking up the phone to call her friend when the next message began. Maybe Tansy was ready to talk about whatever had been bothering her.

Ripley quickly shouldered aside the thought that Ida Mae's death and Tansy's problems seemed to have coincided.

The machine beeped and played back another familiar voice. "Caroline, I—" She deleted her father's message with a vicious stab and was about to cancel the playback when Cage's voice boomed out from the cheap speakers.

"Ripley? Are you there? Please pick up if you are."
There was a pause, and her finger hovered over the delete
button as her inner muscles clenched around the place
where his fingers had been. She had wanted, needed the
release she'd found with him. But it couldn't happen
again. Cage, it seemed, was a new weakness she would
have to fight. "No? Well, call me when you get home so
I know you got there safely. Please? I need to know you're
okay, and I want to talk to you." He rattled off a phone
number and it surprised Ripley that it was unfamiliar.

How could she know how he tasted, yet not know his
number?

The machine replayed a sales call that she promptly
cut off. Ripley's face burned as she remembered just how
intimately she knew Cage now. What had possessed her?
She didn't *do* things like that. Not with the men she usually dated—though "usually" was being generous—and
certainly not with a man she'd just met. A man she wasn't
even sure she liked.

But she'd *wanted* to do it. Needed to touch him. Taste
him. The feel of his velvet steel in her mouth had been a
bigger turn-on than the most expensive candlelit dinner
or the most beautiful moonlit night.

And they'd been in a broom closet! Her clothes stank
of cleaning solvents. Ripley smothered a sound that was
halfway between a laugh and a sob and jumped when the
phone in her hand began to ring.

She answered it automatically. "Hello?"

"Caroline, I—" It felt good to be the one who cut the
connection, and Ripley felt a spurt of power. She'd had
enough of her father's interference. In fact, she'd had

enough of her father. He and Leo wanted the Hospital of the Year? Well, they could go to hell with the award for all she cared.

The phone rang again almost immediately, and she answered it. "Father, we are not—"

"Do you believe in angels, Ripley?" The whisper was soft, ethereal, neither masculine nor feminine. A shiver started somewhere in Ripley's belly, where her muscles still ached from Cage's touch.

"Who is this?"

"They walk among us, you know. Not the ones who died at peace, but the other ones. The angry ones that God forgot. We see them every day, but we don't really *see* them, do we?"

"How did you get this number? It's—"

"Unlisted. I know." There was satisfaction in the words, and a wistful note. "Don't be frightened. I mean you no harm. I'm on your side. I only want to help them. But Cage…Cage doesn't understand. You must stay away from him, Ripley. You must. He'll ruin everything."

Though she wanted to hang up, Ripley couldn't bring herself to cut the connection. There was pain in the whispered words, and a familiar cadence she couldn't place. "Who is this?"

There was a pause, then the barest hint of a whisper. "I'm a friend, with a warning. Get rid of Cage and stop your investigation…or die."

Ripley stared at the phone for a handful of heartbeats while the fear and the awful shivering wrongness of the voice on the phone fled through her and left her empty. Alone.

Afraid.

The sudden peal of the doorbell made her jump, and Ripley froze. Oh, God. Her eyes skittered to the window, where a single feeble streetlight battled the rainy gloom.

The doorbell rang again, and then the knocking started, followed by a voice. "Ripley? Open up, it's me."

"Cage!" She unlatched the chain and opened the door, helpless to do otherwise, though she knew he was almost as dangerous as the shadowy voice on the phone.

She, who prized her independence, could fall for Zachary Cage and bind herself to him as surely as her mother had been bound to her father. And as disastrously.

Weakness. He had become her weakness.

The porch light threw his face into exquisite relief, a study of light and shadow, with shadow taking the upper hand. The rain slicked his hair to his wide brow and plastered his shirt to the chest she'd kissed an hour ago. There was no unfamiliar car in the drive, and she wondered how long he'd been walking.

"I never knew she was sick," he said, and his voice cracked as though he hadn't spoken in days. "She didn't want to worry me, so she went to the doctors alone and never told me about it. Her sister took her to have the lump removed from her breast, and her mother drove her to the first radiation treatment. She told the doctors something was wrong when the burning started, but they prescribed lotion and sent her away. Nothing could be wrong. The linear accelerator's programming was flawless. But they lied." His voice was flat now, deadly.

Ripley sucked in a breath as his black eyes pierced her with echoed pain. She remembered the stories of the women who had died from the software bug, treated with fatal doses of radiation when just a little would have saved their lives.

"Cage." She reached out a hand to him as he stood in the rain and bled from old wounds. But he wasn't finished.

"She finally called me two days later. I was at a dinner and said I'd call her back." He turned his face up to the sky as though the rain could wash away the memory. "The plane home was delayed half a day by weather. I called everyone I could think of. Her family. The doctors. Everyone. But she kept getting worse. I barely made it home before she died." He stepped back until the shadows almost swallowed his tall silhouette. His voice came from the darkness. "I shouldn't have come here, Ripley. But I'm sorry about before, about what I said. I guess…I guess I thought you deserved to know about her. About Heather. I thought you should know that I failed her."

A flicker of lightning showed him walking away when Ripley found her voice and raised it over a grumble of thunder. "Cage!" When he turned back, she opened the door wider and gestured with the telephone. "Come inside."

Chapter Eight

Cage stepped into the cozy apartment he'd followed her to just the day before. The simple elegance of the glossy mahogany furniture and green plants made him feel worse.

She deserved better than a broom closet and another woman's name.

"I'm sorry," he repeated, but she didn't respond any more than she had during his explanation. She just stood there with his dripping jacket in one hand and a cordless telephone in the other. "Ripley?"

She looked at him and the warm brown of her eyes punched him in the heart. "Oh, Cage. I'm so sorry." Her warmth reached out to him. Humbled him.

Had he thought her cold? Unfeeling? How wrong he'd been. She felt each one of her patients' pains, each of her father's careless cruelties. And now she looked like she might cry. For him. It had been a long time since anyone had thought Cage worthy of tears.

He touched her cheek. "Hey. I didn't tell you about Heather to make you sad. I just thought you deserved to know." And he'd wanted her to understand why the explosive chemistry between them could go no further than it had. He was damaged goods. He had been a poor husband back then and would make an even poorer one now. He was five years away from the game. He'd gone back to school and made a new direction for himself. These days he lived a temporary existence, moving from hospital to hospital in search of the next target, the next group of irresponsible doctors to punish.

His life now was one long road trip, without the benefit of a team or the occasional home stand. And as he began to trust Ripley, to see that she was different from the others, he realized she deserved better than that. So much better. She needed his protection right now, not his suspicion.

Not his aching, confused heart.

She shook her head. "It's not just the story, Cage. It's worse." She held the phone out to him as though it was alive. "I just got a phone call."

The simple words shouldn't have summoned a sick twist of dread, but he felt it clench in his stomach at the words and the look on her face. The killer had called. He knew it.

She nodded at the question in his eyes. "He…she, I couldn't really tell. Whoever it was said I was dead if I didn't make sure the investigation failed." She tapped her fingers against her lips. "Come to think of it, Leo Gabney said something similar, only he just threatened to fire me."

Her tone struggled for light, but Cage could see the deep fear beneath. He recognized it in himself, as well.

"Damn it!" The worry gave wings to anger. "What the

hell's going on in your hospital, Ripley? And don't tell me nobody suspected a thing until we noticed that Ida Mae was contaminated. That's bull and you know it. What's been happening in R-ONC? You've had five hot bodies in the last six months—don't tell me you never suspected a thing!"

Cage was shouting and he didn't care. All the emotions of the past few days rocketed through him, leaving him searching for an outlet. Any outlet. The guilty, edgy desire he felt for Ripley was all churned together with memories of Heather and the telephoned proof of a stalking killer. He loomed over her, not caring that a moment before she'd been ready to cry for his pain. He didn't want her tears, or her sympathy.

He didn't know what he wanted from her, but it sure as hell wasn't pity. He caught the scent of sex on her, and flared his nostrils, realizing he wasn't quite in control. The thought made him even madder.

"What do you know about the nukes in the broom closet, Ripley? Don't tell me Leo doesn't know more than he's telling. He knows. Your father probably does, too. That's why they want this kept quiet. They have their priority, don't they? They want Boston General to be Hospital of the Year, whether or not the patients survive it." Memories of Albany Memorial hissed from the shadows, reminding Cage that hospitals were not always the benevolent healers they claimed to be. "But what is your priority, *Dr.* Davis? You know something, or you wouldn't have gotten that phone call. Tell me."

All traces of sympathy gone, Ripley's eyes shot amber sparks at him. "I don't know anything, you baboon." She punched him in the chest and he grabbed both her arms to keep her from swinging again and connecting somewhere more important. She squirmed, bringing their lower bodies into close contact as anger sparked from both of them, promising a conflagration.

He realized, suddenly, that he was as afraid for her as he was of her. Afraid of what she might make him want, what might happen to his goals if he gave in to temptation and took the fall.

For an instant, the image of a broken glass rose hovered around the edges of his mind. Then the feel of her soft body against him all but derailed Cage's thought process. Her scent, sultry and feminine overlain with a hint of sharp, wicked sex, fogged his brain and he shook her, trying to hang on to a thread of sanity. "Tell me, Ripley. What do you know about the radioactivity?"

"I don't know a thing," she snapped.

He saw the denial in her eyes and thought he saw secrets beneath, but didn't wait for the words before he muttered, "Oh, hell," and leaned in.

And quick as taste, he realized rage wasn't the only outlet for his churning emotions after all. Ripley was.

Her lips tasted of anger and forgiveness, a potent combination that sucked Cage into the whirl of sensation he'd come to expect yet still wasn't prepared for. The power whiplashed through him, and with it a sweetness that was born when he'd realized the difference between a doctor and a healer. She cared, he knew. Perhaps too deeply. Just as he could come to care for her. Deeply. Unwisely.

Because a man who lived on the road had no right to love anyone. He'd learned that the hard way.

"Wait!" He drew his head away and heard the thunder of blood through his veins. She deserved better than a man who had failed the woman he loved. "Ripley, I don't… I can't give you what you need." He could give her passion, yes. He could give her his body, but that was all he had to give. And she deserved more.

The desire hummed between them, undeniable and unwise.

"Say my name again," she demanded, and he groaned as she raked a thumbnail across the damp fabric of his shirt.

"Ripley."

She nodded, caught his hand and brought it to her face, where the needs battled with the shadow of fear. That lust and nerves could coexist at all baffled him, but he felt it in himself as he saw it in her. Worries twisted with greed until the tension was unbearable. "That's all I'll ask you to give me, Cage. That's all I need from you. All I want."

But as he sank into her mouth and felt her tongue twine about his like a long-lost friend, Cage wondered whether it would be enough for either of them. Then he didn't wonder anymore. The achy frustration left over from earlier reared up and claimed his body with a roar, and his hands streaked across her torso, relearning places he'd only begun to explore.

She fell back in surrender now as his lips raced across her face and neck. Her fingernails dug into his shoulders when he bent his head and claimed one taut nipple with his mouth. He felt the power of it. The glory. And he damned the outside world to hell for the next few hours.

He needed this. Ripley needed this. The rest of the world outside the dark windows would have to wait.

As if in answer, a pager shrilled.

Her head snapped up, she went on full alert and reflexively slapped at her hip. "Mine?"

"Nope, mine." Heart pounding on two levels, Cage glanced down at the display. No emergency code. Just a local number he vaguely recognized. "Whistler, I think."

Ripley untangled herself from his arms and checked her own pager. "Nothing here, so it's not a patient." Then she stood there in front of a flight of stairs that he guessed led to the bedroom. And waited.

How many times had he put his work ahead of Heather? He'd lost count a long time ago, and hoped he'd learned his lesson. The internal battle was fierce but short. He didn't believe the killer would strike at her apartment, not with him there. And he'd asked Security to double the walk-throughs of the Oncology patients' area.

He'd done his best for now. Until they spoke to Gabney again and convinced him to call in the cops, it would have to be enough. Without another glance at the display, he rehitched the pager on his belt and crossed the room.

He cupped her face in both palms. "Are you sure, Ripley? I don't think I have another ''til death do us part' in me."

She linked her hands around his wrists and stood on tiptoe to touch her lips to his. "Then isn't it lucky for both of us that I don't believe in happily ever after? I'm not looking for forever, Cage. This is enough for me. Tonight is enough."

He might have asked her to explain, but she took him under with just her lips and the caring that seemed an integral part of her. Cage felt the hope and the sweetness flow through him and he didn't ask again. He simply swept her up in his arms and carried her to the bedroom, which was dappled in yellow light from the single streetlamp outside.

If the hairs on the back of his neck shivered to attention as he passed a dark, empty window, he blamed it on the butterfly kisses she rained on his chest. If the splash of the rain against the glass made him shiver, he blamed it on his damp clothing and the chill of the night.

But as they fell to the bed together, he kept his cell phone within easy reach and had a brief moment of wishing it was something else. Like a gun. Then he didn't think anything more. He simply felt.

Where before it had been flash and fire and the naughty thrill of being in a Boston General maintenance closet, now there was time for a soft touch and sigh, though there was no less urgency. They wrestled with his soggy clothes and hers, and the tangled blankets that seemed to have minds of their own. When at last they were naked and touching from nose to toe, Cage let his eyes drift shut as they kissed.

"Say my name," she whispered.

He opened his eyes and chuckled. "I know exactly who I'm with, Dr. Davis. Ripley. Don't doubt it." And he took his lips on a quick foray that had her gasping and fisting her hands in his hair while the air in the room seemed to thicken almost to steam. Then it was past time for gentleness and sighs. The edgy tension in his gut had

Cage rolling to straddle her, lifting her up so they could twine around each other, trapping his aching desire between them until the friction of their bodies was beyond maddening.

"Cage. In the drawer." She gestured and mumbled something about Tansy being optimistic in loading up the bedside table. When he found the stash of condoms, Cage decided to kiss Ripley's best friend the next time he saw her.

While he was fumbling with the slippery packet, Ripley tasted him as she had earlier that day, leaving him trembling on the edge of control. Then it was her turn to tremble as he teased her, sliding the tip of his engorged member back and forth across the dewy lips of her womanhood without venturing inside. She arched against him and opened herself fully, raking her nails across his shoulders when he continued the sweet torture.

"Cage!"

He sighed her name while he eased inside inch by torturous inch, as the shadows outside whispered at the edges of his mind, warning him. Taunting him. He ignored them and murmured hot promises against the side of her neck as he relearned the feel of a woman's body and learned the special feel that was Ripley alone. He'd meant to set an easy pace, but when she spread her legs and arched to take him deeper and deeper still, all intentions of slow lovemaking were erased and he drove into her as he'd wanted to earlier that day.

Hell, as he'd wanted to since their eyes had first met.

"Ripley." He repeated her name again and again like a prayer, not knowing whether it was for her sake or his, and when she locked her legs around him and he felt the first clenching pull within her, Cage followed her down into that long, sweet, burning spiral. And it was like coming home.

AFTER YEARS OF TRAINING herself to wake up at the first hint of noise, usually after only a few hours of sleep, Ripley was disoriented when she woke slowly the next morning and saw the yellow light of morning out the window. Was she sick?

Then she remembered everything. Ida Mae. Mr. Harris. The broom closet.

Cage.

A quick catalog of her body yielded a few unfamiliar aches and the heavy weight of someone else's arm across her waist. Not sick, precisely, but probably unwise. Then a sad smile touched her lips. They'd been "unwise" twice more during the night, and though it was time to deal with that awkward, "Well, I'll call you," moment, she couldn't bring herself to regret the experience.

Her parents' relationship had taught her not to expect poetry and undying love, but she'd been surprised during a string of brief, unlamented relationships to find that not only was love a myth, sex wasn't all that wonderful either. She'd thought it was her. Now she knew better.

She moved to give the arm across her waist a fond pat and was surprised to find that their fingers were tangled together. When she tried to pull away, his grip tightened.

"Not ready to wake up yet," he mumbled, and pulled her back until they were curled together like a pair of question marks. Their linked hands curled across her chest and he nuzzled sleepily at her neck. "Much better."

Part of Ripley wanted to jump up and run all the way to the hospital, where she could avoid the conversation that began, "I really like you, but…" She wished she could keep her memories of how he'd looked into her eyes the moment he climaxed, letting her know that he was with *her,* and nobody else. She wished she could hold on to the way their skins had touched and their breaths had mingled as they pushed each other up and over the edge. But this wise part of her knew the moment would soon come when those memories would be tainted by his inevitable withdrawal.

Then there was another, unwise part of her that nestled a little closer to him in the warm cocoon of blankets and held his hand a little tighter, liking the feeling of safety the simple gesture gave her. That part of her wished the morning would never end. And it was that part that had her rolling over and kissing him on the lips when he said her name as though it was time for them to have *the discussion.*

He let her set the pace, a slow joining in the golden light of morning that had her mind screaming *unwise!* even as her body reveled in the slide of skin and the scrape of teeth. And when the end came, Ripley felt a part of herself pour into him. Felt a piece of him lodge in her heart.

And knew for sure this had been a terrible mistake. She couldn't afford emotion. Couldn't afford weakness.

Couldn't afford Cage.

They lay together, sweat cooling on their skins, hands still linked above his heart, and Ripley grappled for something sophisticated to say even as she feared his first words.

She was saved by the bell. Or rather, by her pager.

Halfway across the room to grab her own unit, Ripley realized that Cage's beeper was howling for attention as well and her heart sank. Her pager showed only a hospital extension, and she was reaching for the phone when it began to ring.

She hesitated a moment before picking it up, half afraid that it was the same sexless voice from the night before. When her beeper shrilled again, she clicked the telephone receiver on. "Dr. Davis."

"Rip, you've got to get down here right away." The relief of hearing Tansy's voice was short-lived as the tension in the other woman's voice registered.

"What's wrong? Not Milo." Please, not Milo.

"No. It's Mrs. Cooper. She's dead, and the Rad Safety goon squad has sealed the room." Tansy paused. "Ripley, I was in there with her just before she died, but I *swear* nothing was wrong. She was happy and chattering away."

Ripley's heart fell to her toes. Janice Cooper, with the jet-black hair and the daughter who'd just had a baby, was dead. And most likely, she was hot as well.

Oh, God. She pressed a shaking hand to her forehead. While she'd been tearing up the sheets with the new RSO, one of her patients had died. R-ONC was self-destructing while she was indulging in a little rescue fantasy.

Well, she didn't think Cage could save her from this one. With another unexpected death so close to the last, and both bodies hot, Gabney would have no choice but to call in the authorities. And R-ONC, like her career, would be history.

But at least no other patients would die. Ripley nod-

The Harlequin Reader Service® — Here's how it works:

If offer card is missing write to: Harlequin Reader Service, 3010 Walden Ave., P.O. Box 1867, Buffalo NY 14240-1867

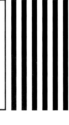

NO POSTAGE
NECESSARY
IF MAILED
IN THE
UNITED STATES

BUSINESS REPLY MAIL
FIRST-CLASS MAIL   PERMIT NO. 717-003   BUFFALO, NY

POSTAGE WILL BE PAID BY ADDRESSEE

HARLEQUIN READER SERVICE
3010 WALDEN AVE
PO BOX 1867
BUFFALO NY 14240-9952

GET FREE BOOKS and a FREE GIFT WHEN YOU PLAY THE...

Lucky 7

SLOT MACHINE GAME!

Just scratch off the silver box with a coin. Then check below to see the gifts you get!

YES! I have scratched off the silver box. Please send me the 2 free Harlequin Intrigue® books and gift for which I qualify. I understand I am under no obligation to purchase any books, as explained on the back of this card.

382 HDL D2AU   **182 HDL D332**

FIRST NAME	LAST NAME

ADDRESS

APT.#	CITY

STATE/PROV.	ZIP/POSTAL CODE

7	7	7	**Worth TWO FREE BOOKS plus a BONUS Mystery Gift!**
🍒	🍒	🍒	**Worth TWO FREE BOOKS!**
♣	♣	♣	**Worth ONE FREE BOOK!**
🔔	🔔	🍒	**TRY AGAIN!**

www.eHarlequin.com

(H-I-08/04)

DETACH AND MAIL CARD TODAY!

ded into the phone and forced the words through a constricted throat. "I'm on my way." She grabbed a suit and shirt from the closet and headed for the bathroom. She ran headfirst into Cage, who was just coming out.

She'd all but forgotten he was in the apartment.

"Oh!" She put out a hand to steady herself and touched warm, bare flesh. Jerking away, she stood, awkward in her nudity and intent on her need to get to work.

"Ripley." He caught her face in his hands and forced her chin up. "Look at me." He waited until their eyes met and held. "It's okay. We'll figure it out together. I'm on your side."

Her prior experiences warred with the desire to believe in Cage. She linked her fingers around his wrists. "Why?"

Touching his brow to her forehead, he said, "Because I trust you, Ripley. If you say you don't know anything about the radioactivity, then I believe you."

"I don't know anything about it." She blew out a breath. "God, I wish I did."

"I know." He kissed her nose. "Me, too, but we'll figure it out together, okay? Now, go get dressed. I'll take a cab home for a change of clothes and meet you at the hospital." He was halfway down the hall before he turned back. "And Ripley?"

"Yes?"

"Be careful, okay? Just keep yourself safe and we'll talk about the rest of it later. Got it?" His bold gaze let her know exactly what "the rest" entailed, but Ripley wasn't dreading the conversation quite so much anymore.

She nodded. "Later." And as she pulled on the clever navy suit that always made her feel in control, she thought that if happily ever after was impossible, maybe she and Cage could shoot for happily for a while.

Maybe.

WHEN RIPLEY REACHED the patients' wing, the hall outside Janice's room was crowded with people, most of whom had no business in R-ONC other than nosiness. Ripley snapped, "I want this area cleared of nonessential personnel right now," and helped a few stragglers along with pointed references to their department heads and the need for heavier workloads if they had spare time to gawk.

She was good at covering her insecurities with a snarl.

That left her with Whistler, Tansy, the two nurses who had been on duty when the patient died, and Belle, who Ripley hardly classified as "essential personnel."

"Mrs. Cooper was one of yours, wasn't she, Belle?" The volunteer tended to pick a few favorite patients, like Milo, for special attention. Ripley figured the older woman was lonely, and she tried not to draw too many parallels between Belle and a R-ONC who slept beside her patients' beds.

"She was a lovely woman, Dr. Davis." Belle's fingers fluttered to her throat. "So strong in her faith, and so happy that her daughter was coming to visit with the new baby. She was so happy. So peaceful."

Ripley thought back to the glow in the new grandmother's eyes when she'd passed baby pictures around just the previous day. Now she was dead. Ripley bowed her head and murmured, "Thank you, Belle. You can keep going with your duties now."

Dismissed, Belle left with one last glance at the closed door and the distinctive black-rayed symbol slashing across it.

Radioactive.

"What's the situation?" The gruff voice came from just behind Ripley, and she forced herself not to react when her heart gave a glad leap in her chest.

"Cage." She acknowledged him with a nod and felt her face heat when one of his dark eyebrows lifted in a silent, private "hello."

A quick indrawn breath from her other side alerted Ripley that the exchange had not gone unnoticed, and she shot Tansy an apologetic glance that said, *we'll talk about it later.*

Much later. After she and Cage had figured out exactly what *it* was and what they were going to do about it.

Whistler answered his new boss, "White female, sixty years old, undergoing implant radiation treatment for breast cancer. The patient had a cardiac incident around nine this morning and was unable to be resuscitated. No medical history of heart problems, no known complications."

Ripley glanced at Whistler. His presentation was as good as any rotating student. She wondered where he'd gone to med school and how he'd ended up a lowly rad tech.

Whether he resented it. Why he'd been at the hospital over the weekend. Twice.

She sucked in a breath and Whistler looked over at her. Their eyes locked, and something hard and mean shifted in his. She took a step back.

"Same sort of contamination?" Cage asked.

Whistler nodded and his eyes went neutral. He turned his back on Ripley and her heart thundered. Had she imagined the moment? She couldn't be sure. The tech answered, "Yep. Blood rather than surface. This time, though, there are nukes in the IV line and on the injection port."

Cage swore and his eyes met Ripley's. They had found their hard evidence. But Janice Cooper, with her crocheted baby sweaters, had died to provide it.

It was too great a cost, Ripley thought, feeling tears threaten. Tears for herself. For a new grandmother. She was tempted to give in and cry, though tears were a weakness. *Guess what, Father?* she asked the voice inside her head, *I'm feeling weak.*

Whistler sidled over to Cage. She could just hear him murmur, "I need to talk to you. It's important."

Cage nodded. "I'll meet you in Rad Safety when I'm done here."

With another quick glance in her direction, Whistler headed for the elevators, leaving Ripley with a very bad feeling. "Cage, I don't—"

But before she could finish, Tansy pressed a folder into her hands. Ripley glanced at the first page and read halfway down before she realized she was looking at Ida Mae's autopsy report.

"Cage." He was at her side instantly, his nearness settling and unsettling her even as she scanned the sparse details. Like any good scientist, she shoved aside suspicion in the face of hard fact.

"See anything?" Cage asked. His breath tickled the back of her neck, reminding her of the many places his mouth had been the night before.

She shook her head, trying to banish the memory and concentrate on the report. "Evidence of pain meds, but that's to be expected. The rest is all normal."

Cage swore. "And no evidence of smothering or strangling. So what killed her if not the radioactivity?"

Glancing at the closed, marked door, Ripley thought out loud. "She'd been dead for some time before we realized she was contaminated, then the autopsy was delayed until the proper shielding could be arranged. Perhaps it was something that metabolized quickly, or broke down right away after she died."

"A chemical with a short half-life," Cage agreed. "That makes sense." The brush of his body against her back was subtle but potent, acknowledging her idea and reminding her of their new partnership. Their relationship, which complicated as many things as it solved.

Cage turned toward the head nurse, hovering nearby. "Shield yourself and draw blood from Mrs. Cooper right now, please, and have the lab test it for everything imaginable. Remind them to keep the sample shielded and call us to decon the room afterward."

The nurse nodded and disappeared, leaving Ripley with half-formed suspicions and no real evidence. "Cage. There's something you should know. I—"

The pager on his hip beeped to life. He glanced down and grimaced. "Whistler again. He said he's got something to show me. Guess my little lecture about job responsibilities really stuck." He returned his attention to Ripley. "Never mind. You were saying?"

She shook her head, feeling foolish. This was *Whistler*

they were talking about—midtwenties, crew cut and a single earring. Hardly dangerous. Her mind was playing tricks, seeing shadows where there weren't any. Seeing "ever after" in what could only be temporary. She blew out a breath. "Never mind. You go ahead and meet with Whistler. Just…be careful, okay?" She stuffed her hands in her pockets, wanting to touch him but knowing it was neither the time nor the place for a goodbye kiss.

Cage must have felt it, too, for his gaze lingered on her lips for a moment. "I'll meet you in your office once I've met with Whistler, and we'll decide where to go from here."

Ripley wasn't sure if he was talking about their investigation or their lovemaking, but she nodded yes to both. "Later." And she turned so she wouldn't give in to the temptation to watch him walk away.

"Into your office. Now." Tansy grabbed Ripley's arm and aimed her toward the inner doors. "What the hell happened while I was away?"

As she collapsed into her desk chair, Ripley couldn't decide whether to laugh or cry. She let her head thump onto the desk and said, "Where do I start?"

"With Cage, of course. Come on, tell me everything." Tansy leaned back and crossed her arms. Her face was clearer today, happier. Ripley sensed that whatever had worried Tansy was now past, and she breathed an internal sigh of relief. Granted, suspecting Tansy was even sillier than suspecting Whistler, but still…

Someone had killed the R-ONC patients. Someone she knew.

Someone she trusted.

IN THE RAD SAFETY OFFICE, Cage gestured Whistler to a chair opposite his. "What've you found about the four other patients on the list I gave you?"

Whistler flipped through a leaning pile beside the techs' computer, shifting the green logbooks to one side and unearthing a folded printout. He scanned the leftmost column. "Including Janice Cooper, who fits the pattern, we have contamination found in six white female R-ONC patients between the ages of fifty-five and sixty-nine. Two were being treated for ovarian cancer and four for breast cancer. All died unexpectedly, though the unexpected death reports list cardiac arrest and cite 'natural causes.'"

"That just means there was nothing obvious in the autopsy," Cage observed. "And why the hell didn't Dixon notice they were hot? Especially after he found that jar of nukes in the broom closet, he should've set up sweeps."

Whistler shrugged. "I wouldn't know, sir." He shifted in his chair and pushed the logbooks toward Cage.

"I'll call him again," Cage said. "He's going to have to talk to me sometime." Though his first impression had been that the former Radiation Safety Officer was nothing more than a skirt-chasing slacker, it was possible there was something more to the man. Perhaps something devious. He looked up and caught Whistler fiddling with the green binders again. "Was there something else?"

He'd assumed Whistler wanted to discuss the women whose old samples had turned up radioactive. The pattern—white women of a certain age being treated for women's cancers—was deeply disturbing. It brought to mind stories of serial killers working within hospitals.

Sick people murdering a mother, a sister, a lover, over and over again. Nurses. Doctors. Healers who hurt.

Like the ones who'd killed Heather.

No, Cage told himself, *don't go there.* Not all doctors were like that. Just look at Ripley. She was different. The very thought of her brought a tingle of remembered warmth. He wasn't sure what to do about it, but there was something very, very special between them now.

Rather than answering, Whistler spun one of the green logbooks to face Cage and opened it to a page marked with a yellow sticky tab. There were perhaps a dozen of the tabs protruding from the book. Cage's eyes focused on the name at the top of the page.

Dr. Ripley Davis, MD.

He pierced Whistler with a look. "What the hell is this?"

The tech frowned. "The R-ONC logs. You told me to audit them. I even came in yesterday to get them. Isn't that what you wanted?"

"Yeah, but I didn't expect you to find anything." Cage could feel the first licks of blackness at the edges of his heart. "Did you?"

She hadn't lied to him about the radioactivity, he told himself. She couldn't have. She cared for her patients, and in the warm yellow light of their morning lovemaking, he'd believed that she cared for him, too.

The first flicker of panic joined the blackness when Whistler nodded.

"It was well hidden, but yes, I did find some irregularities." He tapped the page again.

"What sort of irregularities? Bad handwriting? Missing dates?" Though he'd expect her to be meticulous in all her work, Cage could forgive Ripley a measure of sloppiness. *Please, let it be an illegible doctor's scrawl.*

Whistler shook his head and inched away from the table as though he was afraid Cage might suddenly lunge for him. "No. Missing shipments."

"Oh, God. How many?" Cage felt the warmth slipping away. But he couldn't grasp the concept immediately. *Not Ripley,* his heart insisted. *She swore she knew nothing about the radioactivity.*

Just like the doctors at Albany Memorial had sworn under oath they hadn't known the linear accelerator's programming was flawed. But they had.

"I'm missing four vials of radioactive material that were delivered to R-ONC over the last year." Whistler gestured at the yellow tabs. "Gray eggs that our records show as arriving never appear in these logbooks."

Lies. Rage swirled in his gut, heavy and ugly. She had lied to him. Cage yanked the book closer and thumbed through, noticing many of the doctored pages seemed newer than their neighbors, as though she'd recently replaced the information.

The night before his audit, perhaps?

"Goddammit!" He slammed the logbook shut and lurched to his feet. Glancing at his watch, he realized Ripley would be waiting for him in her office. Well, good. He had a few things to say to her.

He jammed the logbooks under his arm and slammed the door to Rad Safety. He was going to give Dr. Davis a conversation she'd never forget. Then he was going to shut down her department and tell Leo to fire her.

And then he was going to get nasty.

Chapter Nine

While she waited for Cage in her office, Ripley turned her attention to the stack of files she'd requested from personnel with the ID number her father maintained. He'd have a fit when he found out, but she didn't have the clout within the hospital to get the information. He did.

She'd pulled the files of every member of R-ONC, as well as the Rad Safety techs, on the rationale that whoever had injected radioactivity into Janice Cooper's IV bag had had access to both R-ONC and radioactivity. Most likely, it was someone she knew.

Ripley eyed the leaning stack of folders. Someone she knew. She shivered and looked at the door, wishing Cage would hurry up. Though she was still unsure about him, she couldn't deny that he made her feel safe. Protected. The outer office was empty, and she felt very alone without him nearby.

"Great," she muttered to herself, wincing as the word echoed in her office. "The next thing you know, you'll be setting the dinner table for two even though you know he's not coming home. Get a grip, Davis. You're fine without him. You don't need him." *Liar.*

Ignoring the little voice that thought it knew so much, Ripley pulled Whistler's file from the leaning stack. His real name was Elmer Holyrood, which explained the nickname, but as she read further, her own lips parted in a soundless whistle. Sure enough, he'd spent three years in medical school before dropping out for "personal" reasons. Two years later, Dixon had hired him for Rad Safety, but there was no information as to what he'd done in the interim. No additional schooling. No employment history. The years were a blank.

Ripley frowned. It still wasn't enough. It was a hint, but not hard evidence. Hard evidence was the nukes in Janice Cooper's IV bag. Hard evidence was the sky-high levels of adrenaline the lab had found in her bloodstream. It was possible, even likely, that the other bodies had carried high levels of adrenaline that had broken down after death.

Someone was injecting R-ONC patients' IV bags with a deadly cocktail of adrenaline and radioactivity. The massive dose of adrenaline stopped their hearts. And the radioactivity?

She had no idea. It was crazy, just as the person responsible for the murders had to be.

Ripley shivered and pushed the folder aside. She couldn't do this alone. She was too unsettled. Too weak. But for a change, she found little shame in admitting it. In fact, it felt liberating.

She was reaching for the phone to call Cage when she heard him in the outer office. A smile formed, but it fell away when she saw his dire expression. Her stomach dropped to her toes. What had gone wrong now? Was it another patient? She was halfway across the room when he marched into her office and slammed the door shut hard enough to rattle the blinds.

He bared his teeth and Ripley backed up a pace.

"Cage! What's the matter? What's wrong?" She caught sight of the R-ONC radiation logs tucked under his arm, and heard her tone drop to defensive. "Why do you have my logs with you?"

She had no reason to fear her records, but her stomach dropped and she moved another step away from him.

"Oh, Ripley." There was a wealth of disappointment in the words, a world of accusation and betrayal. Then those soft emotions were gone from his dark eyes, and only anger remained. Once again, he looked like the dark warrior she'd first met—a man who hated doctors, especially R-ONCs.

"Cage. Talk to me, tell me what's wrong." She chanced a step toward him, though his expression was anything but welcoming. "Is there something wrong with the logs?" There couldn't be. She was scrupulous in her records and she rode everyone else in the department to be just as careful.

"Ripley, there are twelve entries that don't match the Rad Safety database. In fact, they look as though they've been changed recently." He glared at her with murder in his eye. "When Whistler checked the records, he found radioactive material unaccounted for. The radioactivity we're finding in your patients came from R-ONC."

The information hit her like a blow, as did the accusation in his eyes. For a moment, shock paralyzed her. Her nukes? Those were *her* nukes in the dead patients? Her records had been altered and she hadn't noticed? How had she missed such a thing?

On the heels of shock came a surge of anger. And how dare Cage roll into her office like a battering ram, spewing accusations and glaring at her as though she was the murderer?

To hell with him.

And yet, beneath the anger there was hurt. He had held her so tenderly in the night. Loved her so well that morning. And now this. She balled her fists at her sides and held the tears at bay. She wouldn't show him weakness now. He'd swept the right aside. "Cage, you don't honestly think I had anything to do with changing those logs, do you?" she asked, giving him one last chance to step back and think about what he was saying. "I thought you believed—"

He cut her off with a sharp, angry gesture, and flipped one binder open to a marked page. "See for yourself."

She wasn't sure which was more hurtful, reading the altered entries with her own eyes and knowing that one of her trusted employees must be a killer, or the fact that Cage had come into her office with guns blazing. She jerked her eyes up to his. "Even after everything that's happened the last few days. Even after Harris, the gas, the chapel and the phone call…" *Even after we slept together.* "You still could think for a moment that I knew about this."

She refused to cry. But, oh, it was a battle.

A muscle beside his jaw ticced. "You said yourself that most of that could be explained away. And I wasn't there when you got the phone call. You could have…" He faltered to a stop, but the message was clear.

You could have made that up.

She had forgiven him for his initial wariness. Rude-ness. She had even forgiven him for calling her Heather. But she would never forgive him for this distrust. It cut too deep.

"Right." Ripley slammed the binder shut. "After I goaded Mr. Harris into attacking me, locked myself in the broom closet with chlorine gas, and faked a panic attack in the chapel, is that it?" She advanced on him, wanting to scream at him. Wanting to hit him, to hurt him for mak-ing her feel this way.

She'd only known him a few days, and had understood from the beginning that the end was only a matter of time.

So why did this hurt so much?

He flinched, but didn't deny her claim. "I—"

"Dr. Davis?"

Cage and Ripley snapped their heads up with identi-cal snarls, and the man in the doorway backed up, star-tled. "I'm sorry, is this a bad time? I could come back later. I just wanted to… I need to apologize to you, Dr. Davis."

Ripley closed her eyes, took a deep breath, and searched for the doctor's calm she'd practiced so long and so well.

It wouldn't come. It was too tangled in her feelings for Cage and the hurt that he'd thought, even for a minute, that she'd harm a patient or cover for lost radioactivity. So instead she drew on her tattered pride, forced the tears away and waved the burly, ashamed man into her office.

"Mr. Harris. Come in, please."

Baseball cap in one hand, Ida Mae's husband edged into the office. "Dr. Davis. I want you to know how sorry I am for what happened the other day. I don't even really remember it. You called to tell me Ida Mae had passed away, and the rest is a blur. The doctors say I tried to hurt you." The lines around his eyes and mouth were deeper than they'd been the week before, and Ripley felt a tearing inside her chest at the stark pain in his face.

If love felt like that, she wanted no part of it. Maybe her parents had the right idea, after all. Maybe she had just gotten lucky, and Cage's mistrust was a godsend in disguise. She could get out of this before she fell in any deeper. She could escape with her heart intact. Mostly.

She shook her head. "There's nothing to forgive, Mr. Harris. Your wife died. Grief takes many forms." She tried to offer the tired-looking man a chair, but he declined. His fingers crumpled the baseball cap, and something about his manner made goose bumps prickle to life on her arms.

He wanted to tell her something. But he was afraid. Ripley didn't think it was possible for her stomach to roil any harder than it already was. She was wrong. "Mr. Harris? What is it?"

"I…I wanted you to know…" He glanced back toward the hallway as though afraid he'd be overheard.

"Know what?" Cage prompted, leaning forward as though he was eager to solve the mystery. But that was a lie, wasn't it? He'd already tried and convicted her.

Harris coughed and twisted the hat in his hands. "That administrator, the bald one who visited me in Psych, said I was drunk, that none of it happened. He said my brain made it up so I'd have an excuse to attack you." Harris stared grimly at his knuckles. "But it's the truth. I got a call the morning after Ida Mae…the morning after she passed. The voice on the phone said Dr. Davis killed Ida Mae. There was more, but I don't remember all of it. Just the voice said she should be punished. I should wait near the elevators in the main lobby near lunchtime, that she always came for coffee then." He glanced up at Ripley. "Sure, I was drunk. But not so drunk that I'd make up something like that."

Ripley swayed as the room spun, but instead of leaning on Cage as she needed to do, she batted his hands away and sank to the couch. She barely heard Harris ask, "It's not true, is it, Dr. Davis? Ida Mae died from the cancer, didn't she?"

Cage's eyes burned her and Ripley knew he was waiting for the lie. Waiting for *sometimes these things just happen, Mr. Harris.* And sometimes they did. But not this time.

Ida Mae Harris had been murdered.

Ripley hugged herself and gave Harris a partial truth. "The autopsy hasn't been completed yet. As soon as I know her exact cause of death, I'll be in touch, Mr. Harris."

He nodded and said an awkward goodbye laced with more apologies. She watched him go, wishing she could do more.

Wishing she could feel less. For him. For herself.

Aching, she turned and grabbed her jacket off the back of her chair. "I'm going home."

Cage's fingers bit into her arm, and she could feel the

barely leashed anger vibrating through him. "The hell you are! We need to talk about this! We need to make a plan and call the police. You're in *danger,* Ripley. You're not going home."

"Oh, so now you believe me?" She didn't yell, but her tone brought him up short. "Well, the hell with you. You lost your claim on me the minute you thought, even for an instant, that I'd fudged those logs. I'm not the doctors who screwed up your wife's treatment, Cage, and I'm not your wife." She yanked the jacket over her arms. "You want to call the cops? Go ahead. Tell them everything and see how well Leo twists it around to make you look like a fool. See how long he drags his feet and how many other patients die while he's tap-dancing around the cops. Is that what you want?"

"Of course not, but—"

"But nothing." Ripley felt her shoulders sag. "I'm tired, Cage. So tired I can barely think. Ida Mae is dead. Janice is dead. I'll discharge the rest of the R-ONC inpatients and reschedule the others. There won't be anyone left to kill."

Except me. The words were left unspoken, but they hung between Ripley and Cage like a tangible force.

He stepped forward and lifted a hand as though he wanted to stroke her cheek. When she leaned away, he let the hand drop. "Then at least stay with me, Ripley. My building is guarded. It's secure. You'll be safe with me."

His place, Ripley thought with a yearning combination of attraction and repulsion. The place where he'd lived with the wife he hadn't yet let go of. Safe? Perhaps she'd be protected from the unknown fiend at Boston General who was killing her patients with injected cocktails of adrenaline and radioactive waste. But she wouldn't be *safe* from the greedy hunger that even now begged her to take his offer. To take him.

She wouldn't be safe from herself.

So she shook her head and stepped away, creating the final distance between them. "Frankly, I'd rather stay with my father."

CAGE WATCHED her go and hated himself for reacting the moment Whistler had shoved those logbooks under his nose. Despised himself for not giving her a breath of a chance to explain. To defend. Hated her for making him question the basic tenets that had driven him the last five years.

Hated her for making him feel. Worry. Care.

"Damn it." He slammed the logs back on her desk, and strode down the echoing corridors to the garage.

She didn't seem to notice him as they weaved their way through light traffic on the Mass Pike, but he didn't think it wise to slide into Howard Davis's gated driveway on her bumper. So he parked across the street and waited. Watched, though he didn't know what he was watching for.

After a moment, a uniformed guard crossed the street with a harnessed, lethal-looking German shepherd at his side. Seeing that the man had come from a clever door concealed in the ivy beside the gates, Cage rolled down the window. "Yes?"

"Mr. Cage, Dr. Davis wants you to go home. She said she doesn't need your help and she doesn't want you here." The guard's tone brooked no argument. Neither did the gun at his hip.

"Apparently so. Did she tell you that her life is being threatened by a murderer at the hospital?"

There was a flicker of response, a lift of one eyebrow and a subtle stiffening of the guard's erect carriage that screamed *ex-military. Dangerous. Good protection.* "No, sir. She did not."

Cage relaxed a fraction, knowing she would be safe within the compound. "Didn't think she would. Look out for her, okay?" He slid a business card out of his wallet and handed it to the guard. "Call me if there's trouble."

"I'm not allowed to do that, sir," the guard replied, but he took the card, glanced at it, and tucked it into his pocket, saying, "She's a nice lady, Mr. Cage. I wouldn't want anything bad to happen to her." And he turned on his heel and returned to the guard station hidden in the ivy wall, the shepherd slinking on his heels like leashed liquid fury.

She's a nice lady, Cage thought as he gunned the engine and fled her father's house. Yeah, a nice lady who was tying him in knots. A nice *doctor* lady. What had he gotten himself into? A murder investigation he couldn't take to the police, and a woman he didn't want to want. A woman who didn't want to want him.

Cage cursed and pulled into a convenience-store parking lot. He punched in a now-familiar number and snarled, "Damn it, Dixon. I know you're there. I got your address from your file and I'll be there in ten minutes with a goon squad if you don't pick up. I need to talk to you. Now."

RIPLEY WAITED FOR Rico to wave from the guardhouse to indicate that Cage was gone before she slid out of her car. She was touched that he'd followed. Touched and vaguely disquieted. What did it mean? Did he still think she was involved with the deaths? Was he following her in hope she'd rendezvous with an accomplice?

Or was he trying to keep her safe the way he hadn't protected his Heather?

Once again, Ripley felt the line between her and his first wife blur and shift. If he had become an RSO to save his wife over and over again, then it stood to reason that he was trying to protect her for the same reason. Penitence.

"My name is Ripley," she whispered fiercely as she walked up the granite steps to the massive front door. "Ripley. Not Heather, not Caroline. Ripley." The mantra soothed her for a moment. Then her father met her in the entryway and her equilibrium fled.

"Caroline."

"Father." There was no embrace, just the knowledge that she'd failed to live up to his expectations.

"What is this I hear about another unexpected death in R-ONC? Really, Caroline. That doesn't make your department look very professional. And it could hurt Boston General's chances in next week's vote. Leo is very concerned."

"He should be concerned," she snapped, then took a deep breath. She needed to tell someone. She couldn't lean on Cage anymore, though the knowledge made her heart ache. So she'd tell her father. Maybe he'd come through for her this once. "Janice Cooper wasn't the second death, Father, she was the sixth. My patients are being killed with a combination of adrenaline and nukes, and whoever's doing it wants me dead. But does the administration want to deal with it? No. Gabney wants to avoid it until after the voting. He says we're making it all up."

For a brief instant, Howard's face changed. For a second, he looked sad, vulnerable, worried, all those things she'd wished for over the years. Then he cleared his throat and it was as though the moment had never happened. He frowned and barked, "I know all about your allegations. I have my sources, you know. But the way I hear it, you forged the R-ONC logs to whitewash the disappearance of radioactivity, and you've invented this ridiculous story to cover up the real truth that you haven't a clue why your patients are dying."

Ripley felt the words like blows. So that's how the Head Administrator was going to spin the story. She should have known, just as she should have known her father would take his side rather than hers. Clutching her coat around her shoulders, she gritted her teeth and refused to give him the satisfaction of seeing her cry. "I'm sorry you feel that way, Father. I was hoping to stay here tonight, but I can see that's not a very good idea. I'll just grab a few things from my old room and go to a hotel, then."

She started up the stairs, halting when he said, "Caroline." His voice cracked on the word, but she didn't turn back. She just waited. He continued, "You'll stay here, of course. And…and just in case there is a threat, Leo and I have decided it would be best to disband R-ONC after the Awards voting. I'll expect you to begin work at my clinic the first of next month. It won't be oncology, of course, but I think you'll find general medicine just as rewarding."

Ripley turned back, and was surprised by the almost pleading look in her father's eyes. He wanted her out of R-ONC, she'd always known that. But there was a new level of pressure here, almost desperation.

Then it hit her. Gabney believed her. He knew there was a killer loose in R-ONC, and he had decided to close the department rather than investigate. *Bastard.* She took a step down, nearer her father. "So that's it? He's just going to let the killer walk with a layoff notice? What about my patients? What about the next set of patients? What about them, Father? Don't you care about them?"

Howard fell back a pace, paling almost to gray. He lifted a hand to touch his left arm, and a faint warning bell went off in the back of Ripley's mind, but she was too angry to hear it. She dropped another step, until their eyes were almost level when she whispered, "Don't you care about me?"

Howard drew back as though he'd been slapped, and paled further. Instead of answering, he turned away. His voice cracked in earnest when he said, "We dine in an hour. I'll expect you to be dressed properly."

The sound of his study door thunking closed covered the single sob that escaped her throat. She turned and hurried up the wide, carpeted stairs to the room she'd grown up in.

The soft orange paint on the walls reminded her of the look on her mother's face when she'd picked out the color, and Ripley longed for those days, when her parents had at least shared the same room once in a while.

She and her mother had been close back then, but time and distance had stretched the bonds thin.

Tears prickled and Ripley cursed, knowing they were as much for Cage as for herself or her parents. Her father at least believed she was in danger, though his answer was to play ostrich and hope the problem went away, as his wife had done.

Cage didn't even believe her.

"You're not going to cry for him," she told herself through a haze of tears. "He's not worth it. You knew from the start that there's no such thing as happily ever after. Doctors and relationships are a bad mix."

Well, she'd show him, Ripley thought as the idea took root and determination washed some of the self-pity away. She'd show both of them—her father and Cage. She'd figure this out herself and bring all of Boston General crashing down, if that's what it took to protect her patients. She dug through the pile of castoff medical journals on her childhood desk, pulled out an old hospital roster and flipped it open to *D*. She slid her finger along until she reached *Dixon, George,* and smiled slightly when she saw the number under "emergency contact."

If anyone knew what was going on in the Rad Safety department, it was the head geek himself. He'd been avoiding Cage, but she had a weapon Cage lacked.

She had breasts.

Ripley pulled out her cell and noticed that both Tansy and Cage had called. She promised herself she'd call her friend back later and deleted Cage's message without listening to it. Nothing he could say at this point would interest her. Not even, "I was wrong. I'm sorry. Forgive me."

She wasn't a big believer in second chances. Her mother had given her father a hundred second chances and he'd blown every one of them by coming home too late—or not at all—from the hospital. Ripley had no intention of following in those family footsteps, even if the thought of never seeing Cage again made her want to curl up in a little ball and howl. She'd get through this alone, somehow. She always did.

Hoping Dixon hadn't moved away as soon as he'd been fired from Boston General, she dialed the number and let it ring. And ring. Finally, his machine picked up. When it beeped, Ripley forced a seductive purr into her voice.

"Helllooo, George." She gasped a girlish breath and made a face as she continued, "Are you there, baby? It's been sooo long since we've seen each other, and I was wooondering—"

"Hello? Who is this?" He sounded harried and not a little annoyed, but at least he'd picked up the phone.

She dropped her voice down to normal. "It's Ripley Davis from Boston General, and don't you dare hang up."

"Oh, Christ, it's you. What do you want?" He paused, and the irritation in his voice shifted to amusement. "Let me guess, you want to know about the nukes I found in that closet, right? Just like that putz who keeps calling me."

Putz? Oh, Ripley realized. Cage. A ghost of a smile touched her lips and she didn't argue the point. "What do you say, George? Want to have a chat, for old times' sake?"

"It'll cost you."

"How much?" Mentally, she went through her bank accounts to see what she could afford.

"Two drinks and three dances. Slow ones."

She winced, wishing he'd asked for money. "Okay, but your tongue touches any part of my body while we're dancing and we're done, George. I mean it."

Dixon chuckled. "Meet me at the Slippery Pole in half an hour," he said, naming one of the less savory bars in the Combat Zone just outside of Boston General. "And dress up nice for me, okay?" He hung up with a kissing sound and Ripley shuddered.

"Eewww." That seemed to cover it. She was never quite sure whether his smarminess was an act or real, but unfortunately, George "The Octopus" Dixon seemed like her best hope. He'd seen the radioactivity in the broom closet, and he knew his former techs. And it wasn't as if she had many other options. Her father had made his priorities clear, as had Leo.

And Cage…well, she wouldn't be calling Cage for help. Not ever again.

A fleeting memory of pressure on her lips and a tug deep inside reminded her of waking up in his arms just that morning. Reminded her of the way he'd loved her, slow and sweet in the yellow morning light. Then the memory of his dark, accusing eyes flashed through her mind, along with a twist of guilt and anger.

He hadn't even given her a chance.

Feeling the first relentless beat of a headache, Ripley peered into a closet full of the collected leftovers of her life for something to wear to the Slippery Pole.

She paired a denim miniskirt she hadn't worn since before med school with a low-cut tight-fitting shirt that had probably fit a lot looser when she'd been a teenager. She glanced in the mirror, decided that fluffing her hair out would be eighties overkill, and stepped into a pair of flats that would add to her speed if she had to outrun Dixon on the dance floor.

Then she sank to the edge of the bed and put her head in her hands. What was she doing? Someone was trying to kill her and she was going to the Slippery Pole wearing slut clothes.

What had happened to the safe, solitary nights she spent talking to her cat and watching documentaries about honeybees? And why did those nights suddenly seem lonely? Why did the thought of a dark-haired stranger on her couch fill Ripley with a poignant mix of anger and longing?

Why couldn't she just say, "Well, it was nice," and move on, as she had so many other times before? Cage was complicated, conflicted. He still loved his dead wife, and he was still trying to avenge her death after all these years.

Ripley didn't want a crusader. For that matter, she didn't particularly want a man. So why was she finding it so hard to banish him from her thoughts?

Love is a myth, she reminded herself, *a weakness.* She'd learned the lesson early and well.

The grandfather clock in the downstairs hall struck the half hour. It was time to leave for her meeting.

Instead, she slid her phone from her bag and hit a speed-dial number she rarely used. The tinny ring at the

Intensive Care

other end of the line sounded once…twice…three times, until she was about to hang up when the call was answered. "Hello?"

The familiar voice brought a huge lump to Ripley's throat, and she had to swallow around it to force the words through. "Mother?" Her voice cracked and she tried again. "Mother, it's Ripley. I need to ask you about something."

Chapter Ten

Though he'd never met the man, Cage picked Dixon out right away from the various uncomplimentary descriptions he'd been given by hospital staffers. With a receding hairline, no fashion sense and a fondness for frothy pink alcoholic drinks, the man slouched alone at the bar seemed a poor hope for crucial information, but Cage was too desperate to be choosy.

After seeing Ripley safe at her father's house, he'd returned to Boston General. He'd read the personnel files she'd gotten using her father's name backward and forward and nothing had jumped out at him. He'd combed the broom closet, but the mess he and Ripley had made of the little room during their clinch had obliterated any hints of where the radioactivity might have been found or how the bottles of cleaning solution had been rigged to combine at just the right time. And neither the adrenaline sample nor Janice Cooper's body had yielded anything except more questions. He'd set the IV bag aside, but with no access to the police, fingerprint evidence would be of little help.

And then, miracle of miracles, Dixon had phoned him

back and arranged to meet with him at the Slippery Pole. It wasn't Cage's idea of a classy establishment, but at this point he'd walk on broken glass if it meant getting some leverage to solve the mystery and keep Ripley safe.

He shouldered his way between the gyrating bodies and tried to ignore the silicone-augmented flesh jiggling in cages suspended above the bumping, grinding crowd. He blessed the fact that the music was too damn loud for him to make out more than every fifth or sixth word of the lyrics.

The Slippery Pole might not be Cage's idea of a classy dive, but Dixon seemed right at home perched on a narrow bar stool. He saluted with his glass. "Mr. Cage, I presume."

"Dixon." Cage slid onto an empty stool and ordered a beer he didn't intend to drink. "Nice place."

"A personal favorite. You bring the cash?"

"I've got it." True to his reputed form, Dixon had feigned amnesia until Cage got the hint and offered him money. Guys like him gave RSOs a bad name, Cage thought as he pulled an envelope out of his pocket and slid it along the bar.

Then again, he was no saint either. He'd neglected his wife, failed to punish her killers, then when he was given a chance to clean up Boston General, what did he do? He unbent enough to sleep with a R-ONC but not enough to trust her innocence when suspicious documents came to light.

If he'd just taken five minutes to think it through, he wouldn't have jumped all over her like that. He knew she'd never forge radiation records. He knew better, but he hadn't even given her a chance to explain. He'd jumped straight to the accusations, just as her father seemed to do.

Cage didn't like being lumped in with Howard Davis, but he couldn't argue the comparison. He'd be lucky if she ever spoke to him again.

"Ah, and here's the final member of our little party," Dixon murmured, and Cage glanced up, startled. His jaw dropped. Blood thundered in his ears.

And he thought he heard his heart crack.

Ripley pushed her way through the heaving dancers. She was wearing a tight top that molded her full breasts up and in, and a denim skirt that skimmed high on her smooth thighs. Heat roared through Cage, followed by a predatory, possessive anger when he saw how the dancers' eyes followed the slide of her legs beneath that tiny excuse for a skirt.

In an instant, he was across the dance floor. He grabbed her arm and bellowed, "What the hell do you think you're doing?"

She jumped straight in the air. "Cage! What are you—?" Recovering quickly, she fisted her hands and glared from him to Dixon and back. Her chin poked out stubbornly and the aching, exhausted beauty of her face punched him in the gut. "The same thing you are, apparently."

"Yeah, well. I'm wearing clothes." Cage yanked his jacket off and wrapped it around her before he caught her hand and dragged her to the bar. "You're supposed to be at your father's place. *Safe.*" And why the hell hadn't the guard called to tell him she'd left the compound?

She perched on the bar stool. His jacket hung open as she crossed her legs and let the skirt ride high as if to say, *eat your heart out, Cage, and kiss my butt.*

Swallowing a growl, he took the stool on Dixon's opposite side, not sure whether he'd rather shake her or kiss her.

The ex-RSO favored them with a smarmy smile. "Good, good. I see you two know each other. Forgive me for scheduling you at the same time, but I'm a busy man."

Cage scowled at Ripley, who ignored him, and ordered a beer and another pink thing with two umbrellas for Dixon.

He should have guessed her thoughts would parallel his own, and that she'd have more success reaching the ex-RSO. Dixon was the wild card. He wasn't under Leo's thumb anymore, and if anything had been going on in Rad Safety, he'd know about it. He was their last and best source of information.

That is, unless he was the killer. But two deaths in quick succession after his replacement argued against Dixon's guilt. He was too well known for his presence to have gone unnoticed in Ida Mae or Janice's rooms once he'd been fired.

"Here's your drink," Ripley said, nudging the glass of pink liquid in front of Dixon. "Now tell me everything you remember about finding the nukes in the broom closet."

"Nice to see you, too, Dr. Rip." Dixon leered down her shirt. "How's things in R-ONC? I hear Tansy Whitmore isn't dating Metcalf anymore. What a shame. I'll have to call and console her."

"Dixon." Cage's growl was the only warning he'd give the other man. "Tell us about the broom closet."

The other man grinned unapologetically and shrugged. "Not much to tell. I had an…appointment with Nurse O'Connell that day. I was waiting for her in the closet with the lights out."

"That broom closet sure sees some action," Ripley murmured, and Cage snorted, not entirely pleased to have followed in Dixon's footsteps. Then he wondered how many other people had keys to the R-ONC broom closet.

Wondered who might be missing theirs.

Dixon licked his lips. "She liked it when I used my Geiger counter. I'd turn it on and rub the wand all up and down her—"

"George!" Ripley's bellow startled the odious man into a grinning silence.

"Yes, Dr. Davis?"

"Spare us those details and move on."

"Certainly, Dr. Davis." Dixon removed the umbrellas from his fresh drink, licked them one by one with a pointed tongue, and placed them on the sticky surface of the bar before continuing. "As I said, I was waiting for Nurse O'Connell. I turned my Geiger counter on so it could…warm up before she arrived. Imagine my surprise when it redlined immediately." Frankly, Cage didn't want to imagine anything connected to this little worm, but he didn't interrupt and Dixon continued. "I turned on the lights and swept the area, figuring someone had misplaced a contaminated lab coat and the janitors had hung it up in the closet for safekeeping. Instead, I found a screw top specimen jar behind the waxer. It was full of a clear, brownish liquid that registered counts almost off the meter."

"Brownish," Cage repeated as Dixon drained half his pink drink without coming up for air. "What the hell comes tinted brown?"

"Nothing," Ripley answered. "But some of the nukes are dyed green or red, depending on the strength and isotope. Put the two colors together and you get brown."

Cage knew that. He was an RSO, for heaven's sake. But that didn't mean it made sense. "Put the different kinds of radioactive material together. Like in a waste receptacle?"

Dixon nodded and belched. "That's what I figured. It looked like someone had drained a couple of the waste intakes."

"Hell." That's why Whistler was having so much trouble identifying which isotopes had contaminated the bodies. It was a waste mix. Why the hell hadn't he thought of that? Because, Cage realized, he'd been too convinced the nukes must have come from a doctor. Besides, waste nukes were checked and measured at several points on their journey. "So which department was light on waste check-ins that week?"

"Dunno." Dixon shrugged. "I never thought to look."

If there was anything worse than a bad doctor in Cage's book, it was a sloppy RSO. He felt the anger rise and tried to control it. Was Dixon messing with the investigation, or was he truly that bad a technician? Cage wasn't sure anymore. He snapped, "Why the hell not? Did it escape your attention that a jar of radioactive waste hidden in a broom closet might be a problem?"

Ripley signaled the bartender for another pink night-mare and gave Cage a slight shake of the head as if to caution him against getting in Dixon's face. "I'm sure George did the best he could," she said soothingly.

Dixon nodded. "I came flying out of the closet and ran right smack into a bunch of people. I might've said something to them, I'm not really sure. I went for hot suits and shields, but by the time I got back, the jar was gone."

"Did you ever find it?" Ripley asked, pushing the fresh drink toward Dixon.

This time he swallowed it down without removing the umbrellas. "Nope. Two days later, Gabney gave me the option of resigning with a severance package or being fired with nothing. I resigned."

"You didn't bother to fight it? You didn't tell anyone what you found?" Cage asked.

Dixon put his drink aside unfinished. "I have a kid. Jeremy. He lives with his mother, but he's still mine. What happens to him if I can't get another RSO job? It's not worth it. It just isn't. Crusades are for people with nothing to lose." The ex-RSO stood and slung his coat over his shoulders, barely weaving on his feet.

"You're leaving?" Ripley asked with surprise, and he nodded.

"Yeah. I'll take a rain check on those dances, Dr. Davis. Or you could boogie with Cage here. I've had enough excitement for tonight, and frankly, I don't think being seen with you two is very good for my career goals."

Like hospital administrators hung out at the Slippery Pole, Cage thought snidely. Then he wondered. If someone had followed him, he'd led them right to Ripley. Hell.

He squelched the thought and held up a hand. "One last thing, Dixon. Who was in the hall that day?"

"A few of the rad techs that'd been scanning R-ONC. A couple of nurses. Maybe a civilian or two."

"Which nurses?" Cage asked, leaning forward. Someone had removed the nukes from the broom closet between the time Dixon left and the moment he returned with Leo. That didn't leave much of a window of opportunity.

Dixon twitched a shoulder. "I'm not sure. Older ones. Not hot, so I didn't bother to learn their names. One was black and the other one was short. I don't think I'd recognize them again if I fell over them."

Cage thought briefly about sketching the situation for Dixon and seeing if the other man had any ideas, but he was clearly in a hurry to be gone, and gossip was something they could ill-afford. So he pulled out a business card and handed it to the ex-RSO. "Call me on my cell if you remember something, like the nurses' names or anyone else that might be important to my investigating the hots you found in the closet. Okay?"

"Whatever." Dixon winked at Ripley. "See you around, Dr. Davis. Don't be too upset that we didn't get to dance." And he was gone, slithering eel-like through the sea of heaving bodies, leaving Ripley and Cage alone together. The tension rose quickly, a potent blend of hurt, regret and simmering passion.

"Damn," she said, tugging at the skirt riding high on her shapely thigh. "I wanted to ask him about Whistler."

Cage slid onto the stool next to her and glared around until the male sharks that had gravitated toward her bare legs melted back into the human sea. He might have lost his claim on her through his own stupidity, but he'd be damned if he was going to step aside. "He was in quite a hurry to leave. I wonder why? Do you think he knows something more about your patients?"

She shook her head and slid off the stool, tugging her shirt up. "Doubt it." She shrugged out of Cage's jacket and handed it to him. "Well, that didn't tell us much."

She was avoiding his eyes. What did that mean? Was she still angry with him for distrusting her? Was she worried? Scared? Her expression told him nothing.

Instead of taking the jacket, Cage touched a finger to her chin and lifted her face. "Ripley. Look at me."

There was pain in her eyes, and fatigue. The sight drew him in until he felt as though he were drowning. He wanted to promise her something, anything. He wanted to swear he'd keep her safe, that he wouldn't hurt her.

But it would be a lie.

She turned away, breaking the connection as surely as if she'd told him to go to hell. "I've got to go, Cage."

"Ripley. I'm sorry about what I did this morning." He hoped she knew he didn't say the words often, or lightly.

She paused, but didn't turn back. The music changed again to something poignant and wistful, with a slow melody of strings at odds with the tawdry surroundings.

"I should have brought the logs to you and asked you to help me figure out what happened to the nukes. I should have worked with you rather than jumping right down your throat. I'm sorry. My only excuse is that I've been on my own for a long time now. I'm not used to having someone on my side."

Now she turned back, but he still couldn't read the answer in her eyes. They were cloudy and dark with something akin to regret. "I'm sorry, too, Cage. I know you're just trying to do your job. And I want to figure this out as much as you do. Those are my patients that are dying."

"And it's your reputation on the line," he said without thinking, and saw her eyes darken further, this time with anger.

"No, Cage. My patients. I don't care about anything else right now. I just want to stop this monster from killing patients. Period. I'm sorry you still don't see the difference between a good doctor and a bad one, but frankly, I'm tired of having this argument with you. Good night."

He caught her arm before she walked away. "I'm sorry. I don't know what it is about you that makes me say things wrong, or not at all, but there it is. I know you care about your patients. For God's sake, I've seen you with Milo." He let her go and scrubbed a weary hand across his face, wishing he could explain what he was feeling. But the barriers were still too thick, the walls still too high. He ended with a lame, "I know you're a good doctor."

But apparently it was a start. She stayed put and cocked her head. "Does this mean you want a truce?"

Yes, he wanted a truce with her. He wanted a relationship. A lifetime. *No,* what was he thinking? Cage shook his head to clear it of the slow, sweet music and the sight of her legs. He'd been a terrible husband once before. He knew better than to try again. He couldn't do that to another woman. Especially not one he cared for. So he nodded. "Sure, a truce. Can we start with you giving me a lift home? I walked here from my building."

Her lips curved slightly, though the clouds remained in her eyes. "Okay."

He followed her through the dancers and out into the street, gazing at her legs and feeling the hairs on the back of his neck prickle to attention, like there was someone watching.

Someone waiting.

It had stopped raining, but the gutters were heavy with oily water and city debris. He followed Ripley across the wide main street to her car. He was ten steps behind her when he heard an engine race and saw the single headlight approaching.

Way too fast.

His system kicked into overdrive and he yelled, "Ripley, look out!"

He saw a dark motorcycle angle around the corner almost on top of her. The black-clad rider crouched down and the lethal machine sped up.

"Ripley!" Cage charged across the street and grabbed her by the waist. Something popped in his bad shoulder as he dragged her toward safety. The motorcyclist shifted gears with a howl of engine noise just as Cage launched Ripley between a pair of parked cars.

The motorcycle roared past, and was gone in a blast of noise. The echoes hung for a moment, then they disappeared as well. Everything was quiet in the little street. Unchanged.

Shocked, rattled and filled with rage that once again Ripley had been endangered and he'd almost been too late, Cage lay still for a moment as the gutter water soaked through his pants and his shoulder started to howl.

"Cage!" Ripley squirmed and righted herself, dragging a hand through her now-soggy hair. "Are you hurt? Are you okay?"

He struggled to his feet and braced his hand on a nearby car. Too bad for the owner, he thought as he smeared gutter filth across the hood. "I'm fine," he lied as the pain sang down his arm and rage pinched his gut. "Are you okay?"

"Sure." Her too-tight shirt was askew and both her knees were scraped raw, but she seemed otherwise whole.

Cage felt a gush of relief and a profound desire to pull her into his arms and kiss her. To prove to both of them they were still alive. But he'd given that right away. He'd pushed it away with both hands that morning, because it was easier to suspect than to trust.

"Someone just tried to kill us," she stated calmly, though her pulse pounded at her throat and her face was gray.

"Yeah," he agreed, feeling adrenaline and anger warring for dominance within him. He cursed. "Come on, we'd better get out of here before they come back."

"Or we could call the police," she offered, though her voice held little conviction.

"We could," he agreed, "But since Gabney and your father will deny there's anything wrong at the hospital, it'll be a random thing in their books. Just a bit of bad Boston driving, you know?" The knowledge soured in his stomach. Yet again, the administration, the *system* was failing him. Failing his woman.

"You're right." She blew out a breath. "Let's go, then."

They drove to his building in a silence that was tainted

with unsaid things and an edgy blend of leftover hurt and sexual frustration. When the car was stopped, he said, "Why don't you come up and spend the night? I have a guest room, and I'd feel better knowing we were both safe on the top floor, behind a sturdy security system."

She gazed out the windshield. It was raining again, and the water made crazy tracks down the sloping glass. He wished he could read her mind. Wished he knew where they stood. Wished he knew what he wanted. What she was feeling.

Finally, she answered, "No, thanks. Father's mansion is just as tightly guarded. I'll be safe there."

"Ripley, that wasn't—"

"Cage. Don't." Her quiet words effectively silenced him, which was a relief, as he wasn't sure what he'd been about to say. "I can't do this, okay? It was a mistake for us even to try. You're still working through your wife's death, and I'm…I'm not looking for complications, okay?"

"Heather has been gone a long time, Ripley. I do what I do because of how she died, but not because I still love her." It was true, he realized. Her memory was faded by time, and the guilt had even leveled a bit, allowing him to see their relationship as it had been, rather than through the purifying lenses of the survivor.

He hadn't been perfect. But then again, neither had Heather. Or perhaps it was the match that had been flawed from the start, and that regret, more than anything else, drove him harder. In the end, he just hadn't loved her enough.

"I don't put much stock in love," Ripley said, staring

through the windshield. "And I'm too tired to have this conversation tonight. I'll be safe at my father's, and tomorrow we'll meet with Gabney again. After this motorcycle incident, and the evidence we've gathered, he'll have to call the authorities." She shivered slightly, although the car was warm.

"And where does that leave us?" Cage asked, not knowing what he wanted the answer to be, but knowing he didn't want to go upstairs alone.

"When this is over," she answered without answering, "what will you do? Stay here and run the BoGen Radiation Safety department, or take a job at some other hospital where you can save the world from crooked doctors?"

Cage didn't say a word, knowing it was answer enough, and she nodded. "Yeah, I thought so. Which leaves us," she jerked a thumb between the two of them, "a fond memory with no future. So let's not make it harder than it already is, okay?"

"You're right. I don't like it, but I know you're right." Disappointment shimmered through him, only slightly tempered by the fact that he knew he couldn't give her what she needed. He pulled out a business card and scribbled a string of numbers on the back before handing it to her. "Take this. My cell number is on the front, and the security code for my place is on the back. I'll leave your name with the doorman. If you need me for anything, call. And if you need someplace to be safe, promise me you'll come here, okay?"

Their eyes met and held. Her chin dipped in the barest of nods. "Okay. But 'safe' is starting to feel like a pretty relative term. And thanks for pushing me into the gutter.

I'll return the favor some day." She pressed a scraped palm to his cheek before he slid out of the car.

He leaned back in, feeling a new burst of rain hit the back of his neck. "Please, please keep yourself safe, okay? We'll figure the rest out together." He shut the door and watched her pull out of the parking lot, wishing things between them could be different. Wishing *he* was different.

Then he watched a few minutes longer, making sure that no dark motorcycle pulled out behind her. The street stayed empty. But the hairs on the back of his neck stood at rigid attention. There was someone out there. Waiting.

WHEN RIPLEY LET HERSELF into her father's house, the first thing she heard was his bellow of, "Caroline Ripley Davis, where in God's name have you been?" Her father stood in the foyer, and he looked almost…worried.

The nagging fear that had dogged her drive home fled instantly, replaced with a suspiciously warm glow. Howard had been worried about her? He believed she was in danger? He cared?

Barely trusting her voice, Ripley ventured, "I…I was out. I'm sorry if—"

She was cut off by a quick gesture. Howard ran his eyes up and down her body. "You missed dinner. And what are you wearing? Did anyone see you like that?"

The quick slap of hurt stiffened her spine and drove away the warmth. He hadn't been worried for her. He'd been worried for himself, as always. "Yes, I went out in public dressed like this," she replied. "And no, my knees don't hurt too badly, thanks for asking." Pride kept her from limping across the tiled foyer, and stubbornness kept the tears at bay. She should have stayed with Cage after all. Perhaps Howard would have worried if she hadn't come home at all. Then again, perhaps not. She set her foot on the bottom step and called over her shoulder, "I'm going to take a shower and then I'm going to bed."

"Caroline, get back down here! We need to discuss your new position at the clinic, and how you can avoid suits from the Harris and Cooper cases. Malpractice settlements don't look good for the Davis name, you know."

Maybe it was stress and exhaustion. Maybe it was the final insult in a long string of such things. Or maybe it was the added strength she'd gained from holding firm against Cage, who tried to be just as overbearing as her father. Whatever the cause, Ripley felt a sudden crack in the tight control she kept on her emotions around her father.

And the anger, which she'd always dismissed as childish, felt good.

She spun around on the stairs, but stayed two steps up so she'd have the advantage of height, and the wonderful echo of the marble foyer walls. "No, Father. We won't discuss anything. We never do. You lecture and I listen. That's not a discussion."

Howard sniffed. "Well, Caroline. I can see that you're in no mood to be reasonable. We'll talk about this another time."

"Don't you dare walk away, Father!" Ripley yelled, and had the satisfaction of seeing him turn back around, eyes wide. "If you walk away now, I'm leaving here and never coming back. You may not believe I'm in danger, but I'm telling you it's the truth. You either start listening to what I have to say, or I'm out of here. Do you understand me?"

He frowned. "Caroline, really—"

"My name is Ripley!"

In the sudden silence that followed her bellow, Ripley heard a noise from the side-door breezeway. She and her father both turned toward the sound. And froze.

"Oh, goodness." The tall brunette fluffed a hand through her artfully cut hair and hooked a heavy-looking golf bag over one of the marble lions. "I'm not a moment too soon, am I?"

Ripley felt a headache descend with sudden vengeance, and her knees started to throb like crazy. She closed her eyes and wished with sudden ferocity that she had taken Cage's offer. Even staring at the ceiling of his guest room while reliving every one of his touches and balancing them against every one of the reasons why they couldn't be together would have been preferable to this.

But when she opened her eyes, she was still standing on the marble staircase of her father's mansion, and Eleanor Caroline Davis was still in the foyer.

Her father was frozen in place with his mouth hanging open and one hand in the air, so Ripley sighed and said it for him.

"Hello, Mother. Welcome home."

Chapter Eleven

An hour and several aspirins later, Ripley still hadn't made it to bed, though her father had disappeared soon after their family reunion in the foyer. She felt hollow from the emotional highs and lows of the past few days. Empty. Alone.

"So tell me about this man you mentioned on the phone." Clad in silk lounging pajamas embroidered with the name of a faraway country club, Ripley's mother was a study in elegance, except for the hint of a farmer's tan on her arms and nose.

"It doesn't matter anymore." Ripley tried to find a more comfortable position on the couch, but her scraped knees had stiffened after she showered. "I'm not even sure why I called you." Except that she wanted to understand why happily ever after didn't exist, and had thought her mother might know.

Eleanor's eyes clouded. "I suppose I deserved that."

"I didn't mean it badly." Ripley touched her mother's hand. "I meant that it really wasn't important enough for you to fly home in the middle of a tournament." Which was a surprise neither Ripley nor her father had been expecting. "It's over between Cage and me, anyway. We've agreed it's for the best to keep things on a professional level instead of a personal one." Except that her lips still tingled with the imprint of his. She could still taste him on her tongue. Feel him against her skin.

"And the problem at the hospital you told me about? I assume that's what has Howard all in a lather." Not for the first time, Ripley wondered at her parents' relationship. There was no anger in her mother's voice. Only a fond tolerance, and perhaps a hint of something else.

Something Ripley hadn't noticed when she was a child.

"That's still a problem," Ripley allowed. "But I don't want you or Father to have any part of it. I'll handle it myself." By unspoken agreement, neither she nor Howard had mentioned the full extent of the problems to her mother. It was perhaps the first time in her memory that she and her father had worked together, but neither of them wanted Eleanor near BoGen. Ripley wanted her mother safe. Howard just wanted her gone, or at least that was how Ripley interpreted his chilly silence and quick absence.

"Are you sure?" Her mother's touch was gentle, and lodged a ball of sweet memory in Ripley's throat. "I haven't been around much these last few years, but I'm not stupid, you know. If you're in some sort of trouble, let Howard help you. I know he can be heavy-handed in his methods, but your father only wants to fix things for you because he loves you."

Ripley shook her head with a wistful smile. "No. He doesn't want me to make him look bad. Don't try to placate me, Mother. I know the score."

Instead of responding, Eleanor looked at her for a long time until Ripley had to fight the urge to squirm. Finally, her mother said simply, "I *have* been gone too long, Ripley, and I'm sorry. I thought you understood."

What was there to understand? Howard was a tyrant and his wife had gone golfing rather than be around him. That's all there was to it. That was all Ripley wanted there to be, because if there were other factors involved, she might have to reevaluate her own thinking about relationships.

About love. About being vulnerable to a man like Cage.

Suddenly unable to sit there any longer, Ripley climbed painfully to her feet and checked her pager, though both of them knew it hadn't gone off. "I do understand, Mother. And I have to get to the hospital. Will you be here tomorrow?"

Eleanor sighed. "Yes, Ripley, I'll be here tomorrow. Maybe you'll want to talk then."

"Yes, Mother," Ripley said, though she was pretty sure she'd heard it all before. "We'll talk tomorrow."

Up in her room, she dragged jeans over her skinned knees and a sweatshirt over her drying hair. As she snuck out the side door so she wouldn't have to pass her father's library, Ripley thought she heard the murmur of voices from the parlor. Then she shook her head. Her mother must've turned on the small television that was hidden in an ornate cupboard.

The alternative was too unbelievable to consider.

Once outside the main gates, Ripley paused at the crossroads, realizing she didn't have a plan. She'd just needed to get out of the big house. She couldn't go to her apartment because the killer had called there. He knew where she lived. And she couldn't go to Tansy's apartment because it wasn't in a secure building. Besides, it seemed as though Tansy had problems of her own.

The car seemed to turn itself toward the city tower she'd visited earlier that night. The guard at the parking garage let her in without a fuss, though it was close to two in the morning, and the man at the front desk greeted her with a smile and addressed her as "Doctor." The elevator carried her up to the top floor and deposited her in a plush foyer.

At the door, Ripley faltered as she looked around. What was she doing here?

It seemed unbelievable that Boston General's rude, outspoken RSO lived in the penthouse of one of the most desirable buildings in the city. The floor of the elevator lobby was done in dark marble, and the green plants spilling from the tasteful indoor garden probably had a staff of their own. It was, Ripley thought, exactly the sort of place her father would buy if he lived in the city. That alone was enough to spark her retreat.

Her finger was on its way to recall the elevator when she heard the door behind her open.

"Ripley?"

And suddenly it didn't seem so strange anymore, because there he stood, shirtless, with ragged sweatpants hanging off his narrow hips, and he looked like Cage. He didn't look like the multimillionaire owner of several buildings, or the man who'd fought Albany Memorial for justice and lost. He didn't look like the young pitcher in the clippings Milo and Livvy had been passing around, or like the man she imagined had married a woman named Heather.

No, the ragged, tired man holding his hand out to her looked nothing like the person he'd once been, Ripley realized. He looked like the man she'd come to know so well in such a short time. The dusky skin across his chest was etched with strength and lined with muscle. In that moment, she thought she could trust him to protect her from anything. Everything. "Cage," she breathed, finding for the first time that his name seemed stiff on her tongue. Formal.

He seemed to sense it. "You can call me Zachary, if you want. Zack." He stood back from the door and gestured. "Are you coming in?"

Ripley stayed put, feeling as though the small step into his home was inevitable, yet knowing it was the biggest decision of her life. She peered past his outstretched arm, thinking that he had shared the space with his wife.

As though sensing her concern, he took Ripley's arm and led her in. "I gave away most of Heather's things and boxed the rest up. There's not much here now, just a few pieces of furniture and some odds and ends." He paused. "There's not much of Heather in here, but there's not much of me either, Ripley." And she didn't think he was talking about the furniture anymore.

She nodded and allowed herself to be drawn into the penthouse, barely registering the opulent tiling and the understated elegance of the open, airy floor plan. "You hurt me this morning, Cage. What you did really hurt. You should've trusted me more than that."

He nodded, and his eyes darkened to coals. "I know, and I'm sorry. But given the same information, I'd probably do it again, Ripley. My job is to protect the patients from the hospitals."

"There's that honesty," she murmured, and stepped forward in the tiled hallway to cup his cheek in her scratched palm. "I admire you for it, even when it makes me crazy." She touched her lips to his and smiled. "I could use a friend, Zack."

On a shuddering sigh, he dropped his forehead to rest on hers. Close up, his eyes were tired, but clear. "I could use one of those, too, Ripley." He kissed the tip of her nose. "I'm glad you came here. Can I offer you a guest room?"

She didn't want a guest room. She wanted him. She wanted to feel alive for the night. Feel safe, as though the rest of the world couldn't get her. And she knew she'd find that security in his arms. She slid her arms around his warm, bare waist, and noticed that when he returned the embrace, he winced. "What happened to your shoulder?"

"An old injury flaring up, that's all."

She kissed the place where the dusky hair covering his chest gave way to the smooth, tight skin of his sore shoulder and touched her lips to the pale white lines that spoke of old surgeries. "Because you saved me from the motorcycle."

"In part." His breath hitched when she splayed her hand flat across his stomach and kissed his shoulder again. "Ripley..." His voice was a warning growl. "About that guest room."

"Do you believe in happily for a while, Zack?"

"In what?" She could see the flutter of his heartbeat in the pulse at his neck, and felt an answering throb deep within.

She shook her head. "Never mind. And don't bother with the guest room. We can share."

As though he'd been waiting for permission, his mouth swept down to settle against hers. Ripley slid into the kiss on a sigh and wished the rest of the world to the devil as she wound her arms around his neck and held on tight. Who cared about happily ever after?

She was happy *right now.*

IN THE PREDAWN darkness, Cage rolled onto his bad shoulder and woke with a groan. Then he realized he wasn't alone in the big bed and he lay back for a moment, trying to organize his thoughts.

Just twenty-four hours earlier, he'd woken up wrapped around Ripley following a night so intense he had yet to fully process it, or what it might mean. Now, a day later, they were once again lying together, but it wasn't the same. She was turned away from him, curled in a motionless ball that shut the rest of the world out. Though they had loved each other during the night, her needs had possessed a sharp, almost ferocious edge as if she was storing the sensations away for remembering once it was over.

And it would be over soon. Cage could feel the pieces gathering momentum as they rushed to fit together into a whole pattern. The killer had struck twice since his arrival, and the motorcycle attack showed a growing boldness that scared him.

Ripley murmured in her sleep, rolled over and splayed her hand across his bare stomach with an acceptance that was foreign to her waking state. He reached down and brushed a strand of dark hair away from her face, wondering what would become of them when this was over.

Just as Heather's death had fundamentally changed him, Cage worried that this job might mark him as well. And in the dark before dawn, he was afraid he might not have the strength to pick up the pieces and rebuild himself again. He would leave Boston General when the Radiation Safety department was back on track and seek out another struggling hospital, another place where patients' lives were being threatened.

But this time when he left, he'd be leaving a piece of himself behind.

When he slid from the bed, Ripley mumbled a protest but didn't wake. He dressed quietly and assuaged the spark of guilt with a note left on his side of the bed, arranging to meet her at the hospital café for breakfast.

It should have been enough, but as he jogged up the main steps of Boston General, Cage still felt as though he'd taken the coward's way out in not waking her to say goodbye.

She deserved better. But then again, that's why he held himself away. She deserved a whole man, one who would trust her and love her. Protect her.

"Why, Mr. Cage! You're here early this morning, aren't you?"

The feminine voice knocked Cage out of his stupor, and he stared down at the volunteer. "I could say the

same for you, Belle. Are you on your way to see Milo?"
He knew that the boy was a special favorite of hers.

"Yes, I'm on my way now. His parents missed their
visit again, poor thing. But he's so looking forward to the
field trip today."

"Field trip?" Cage asked blankly.

Belle nodded. "Oh, yes. Today is Boston General's day
to use the Tammy Fund's box behind the Boston dugout."
Her brows drew together. "I thought Milo said you were
going with them?"

Cage vaguely remembered the boy asking him to the
ballgame. He remembered telling the kid he wasn't going,
but at the time it hadn't seemed important. It wouldn't be
important now except... "Will Dr. Davis be going?"

"But of course! She's the main chaperone!"

And he'd bet his life that there'd be no talking her out
of it. The likelihood was that this would be one of the last
few times she'd see her patients. Cage just didn't see how
they could protect her department from being shut down
once the murders came to light. So he nodded. "Then yes,
I'll be going to the ballgame."

He hadn't been near a ballpark in five years, ever since
Heather had called him at a Tammy Fund benefit to tell
him that she wasn't feeling well.

He'd told the organizers to take a message. The guilt
still sickened him. If he'd gotten the message sooner,
gotten home sooner...Heather would still be dead. She'd
been dead the moment the doctors had strapped her to the
table beneath the linear accelerator and overdosed her
with radiation measured by a faulty program.

Belle dimpled at his response. "Milo will be so

pleased. Well, I'll be off then." And she was gone before he had a chance to ask why the heck *she* was there at 6:00 a.m.

Ripley had once said she thought Belle was lonely. The volunteer's mother had died years ago, and her father had passed away just recently. She seemed to need the patients as much as they needed her. Perhaps more.

Cage made it halfway to the Rad Safety office before another voice hailed him. "Hey, boss. You couldn't sleep either, huh?"

Whistler was looking cheerful this morning, Cage noted while wondering whether he was the only hospital employee who thought arriving before 9:00 a.m. on a Monday was ambitious. Then he thought, *Whistler.* Had he been one of the rad techs in the hall that day?

They walked to the office together, and as he held the door for the other man, Cage said, "Hey, do you remember when Dixon found those nukes in the R-ONC broom closet?"

Whistler nodded. "Yeah. Why?"

"Who else was in the hallway?"

The young tech cocked his head, considering. "Me and Hiram. Jonesy, too, I think, and a couple of nurses."

Cage prodded, "Which nurses?"

"Lenore from Neonatal Intensive Care, and…I think it was the short one who hangs around with your girlfriend all the time. Why?"

Tansy. Cage identified the second nurse—she was a doctor, but George might not make the distinction—even as his mind balked at the term *girlfriend.* Grown men did not have girlfriends. They had…lovers. Fiancées. Wives. Families.

He clenched his jaw at the spear of regret. He'd done all that. Now he was doing something else. He was keeping the hospitals safe for their patients. It was a higher calling than family, though he was doing it for the family he'd lost.

For the children he would never have.

He turned away from Whistler without answering, needing to be alone for a moment. But when he opened the door to his office, the glint of crimson and crystal stopped him, as did the picture from the *D* page of the Boston General staff directory, slashed and stained red. A collapsed bag of plasma in the trash gave mute testimony that the red liquid was just what it looked like.

Blood.

Below Ripley's shredded picture, trailing off onto the blotter, words were scrawled in the blood.

Do not Interfere With the Lord's Work.

The obscene message and the salty smell turned Cage's stomach. "Damn it! Enough already! Who the hell are you? Come out, you coward. Show yourself!"

"Boss? Everything okay?" Whistler stuck his head around the door, and Cage shifted to block the sight of his desk without thinking.

"Everything's fine. I'll be out in a moment." Was that a gleam of satisfaction in the young man's eye? Cage couldn't be sure anymore. He didn't know who to trust except himself, and that even seemed fuzzy at times.

Ripley. The monster was fixated on Ripley. But who the hell was the monster? Someone in the hospital, obviously. Someone with access to Rad Safety and R-ONC.

Cage snatched up the items and was on his way to

Leo's office before he realized it wasn't even seven in the morning. Leo, for one, wouldn't be in for hours. Cage's stomach roiled with anger and fear. Ripley was a target. They'd known it all along, but the note and the picture brought the problem into sharp relief. Ripley was in danger, and it was up to him to figure out who was threatening her.

He paused when he realized the café was open, and the gift shop. He reversed direction and took the stairs down to the atrium two at a time. The salesclerk in the gift shop jumped when he slapped his hand down on the counter and showed her the broken glass rose stem he'd found on his desk beside a bloodied picture of the woman he'd come to care for against his better judgment.

"Tell me who in this hospital has bought one of these since Friday. And tell me quick."

HALF ASLEEP, Ripley stared stupidly at her cell phone, which was speaking to her with her mother's voice. "Darling, where are you? We were worried."

"Mother?" What was her mother doing on the phone?

Ripley glanced around and realized that the more pertinent question was where the hell had she slept? Then she remembered. Ida Mae Harris. Janice Cooper. Cage. She'd slept at his place and they'd made love. Now it was morning and he was gone.

"I'm fine, Mother," she answered automatically while her sleepy eyes scanned the note she'd found beside her. She supposed she should be grateful that he'd left the note, but the annoyance was quick and sharp. Apparently she only rated cuddling once.

"Where are you?" Eleanor repeated, "We were worried."

"Don't worry, Mother. I'm fine." Ripley wondered whether that was the royal "we" or whether her mother and father were actually doing something together for a change, even if it was worrying about their only child. "Tell Father I will not be working at his practice, and *do not* come to the hospital to visit me, okay?"

Though she and her parents had fought over the years, Ripley couldn't stand the thought of either of them being hurt by the killer stalking her at Boston General. Her father might not want to believe in the danger, but she'd be damned if she'd let him be harmed.

Eleanor sighed. "We really do need to talk to you, dear. When can you come to the house?"

"Not today, Mother. Maybe tomorrow. I have to go now. Bye." Ripley disconnected quickly, before the headache got any worse.

Her parents were difficult enough separately. But together? She shuddered. That was one thing she couldn't deal with right now. She didn't want to speak with them yet, and she didn't want to worry for their safety. She glanced down at the note in her hand again, thinking that Zachary Cage was another thing she'd rather not deal with, as were Leo Gabney, Boston General and the murderer stalking her.

The thought brought a shiver of terror and a sting of pain to her knees, where she'd fallen to the gutter after Cage had saved her yet again.

Thoughtfully, fearfully, she looked around the bedroom and took solace from the solid masculinity of the furnishings and the half-packed boxes around the room. Cage's penthouse felt safe. There were locks on the windows and guards downstairs. She could stay up here forever and be protected.

Then she thought of Mr. Harris's eyes when he'd asked why Ida Mae died, and she knew avoidance wasn't an option. Gritting her teeth, Ripley got out of bed and faced the day. But she couldn't shake the feeling that there was something ominous on the horizon.

She drove to her apartment to shower, resenting the nerves that had her looking over her shoulder and dreading the ring of the phone. She scrubbed her body hard, trying to wash away the weakness before she saw Cage again. It probably would have been best if she'd stayed away last night, but she hadn't been able to deny herself the anchoring stability of his presence, at odds with the hot, greedy rush of need he brought out in her.

"That's all well and good," she told herself, "Just don't think you can depend on him. He showed his true colors yesterday morning." But she dried her hair quickly and jumped into fresh clothing, suddenly in a hurry to reach Boston General, though she couldn't have said why the urgency tapped in her chest. *Get to the hospital,* it said, or perhaps, *get out of the apartment.* She wasn't sure which, but she was on the road to Boston General moments later when her pager buzzed. She checked the display and felt a jolt of adrenaline at the message.

Café. Now.

She hit the lot way too fast and parked. Sprinting across the tarmac and jogging through the atrium left her little breath, but Cage wasn't in the mood for conversation. He met her by the café doors, handed her an enormous carry-out cup and jerked his head up the stairs. "Come on."

"Good morning to you, too," she muttered, though she had promised herself to let it go. "Yes, I slept fine, thank you, except for the part about waking up alone."

Black eyes glanced back. "I left a note."

"Yes, you did."

He turned away after a moment of silence, and shrugged his left shoulder while the right one hung awkwardly. Apparently the "old injury" was more severe than he'd let on. "Do you care where we're going, or are you enjoying your snit?"

"Where. Are. We. Going?" Ripley managed between clenched teeth, wondering why it was so difficult for her to keep things casual between them. Why did she keep wanting more from him at the same time that she wanted to shove it away with both hands?

"Rad Safety," he replied, as though that wasn't obvious from the direction they were walking. "We have a meeting."

"With?"

"A medically trained radiation worker who bought three glass roses the day after you were attacked." He kicked open the door to Rad Safety and Ripley followed close at his heels, wanting to see the young man's face when Cage said with deadly steel in his voice, "Hello, Whistler."

Chapter Twelve

"You paged me, boss?" Was Whistler's innocent expression feigned or real? Cage wasn't sure, just as he wasn't sure how to handle Ripley's volatile mood.

He'd never had to work particularly hard to keep Heather happy. As long as the money kept coming and she had her spot in the wives' box, she was content.

Somehow, Cage doubted Ripley would be that easy. And what could he offer her now, anyway? Either a long-distance relationship or a string of temporary homes while he continued moving from hospital to hospital, cleaning up other people's messes and trying to keep a few more wives and mothers alive.

"Boss?" Whistler's voice broke in even as Cage grappled with the fact that somewhere along the line he'd begun to think of his and Ripley's time together as a relationship. A doomed one, perhaps, but a relationship nonetheless. "You emergency-paged me?"

"Cage?" Ripley poked him in his good shoulder. "Hello?"

"Of course, sorry." Cage sat down and waved her to a chair.

Whistler glanced between the two of them. "This isn't an emergency, is it, boss? What's going on, are you firing me?" He spread his hands. "I know maybe I haven't been the friendliest, but I can try harder. I liked Dixon, you know? He kept things fun, and we didn't have to work as hard as you're making us."

Ignoring that, Cage reached into his coat pocket and pulled out the broken crystal rose stem he'd found on his desk. The anger was quick and fierce. Nobody threatened his woman. Nobody. "What can you tell me about this, Whistler?"

Ripley sucked in a breath and touched her own pocket, where Cage knew she carried the stem he'd handed her the first time they met. He hoped it meant something that she kept the thing.

"It's broken," the young man observed, then his eyes sharpened. "Hey, that's from one of those glass roses! Where'd you get that? I bought three of them from the gift shop the other day! My girlfriend collects glass flowers, you know? It's our third anniversary next weekend and I'm going to tuck them into a bouquet of real roses as a surprise."

That sounded…believable. Cage frowned, disappointment warring with relief. He wanted to find the killer, but he didn't want it to be Whistler. The kid was Rad Safety. He was one of the good guys. "Where are the roses you bought?"

Whistler jerked his head toward the Rad Safety break room. "In my locker, wrapped in a set of scrubs to keep them safe. Why?"

Ripley quickly asked, "What made you leave medical school?"

Whistler blinked in surprise before answering, "My father's parish ran out of money just about the same time my mother was diagnosed with breast cancer. Insurance wouldn't cover the treatments, so I quit school and worked two jobs to keep the family going." The boy glanced down at his hands. "She was only fifty-two when she died. My dad never really got over it, you know? If she'd just gotten better treatment…"

The dead patients were all female cancer patients in their fifties and early sixties. Was the killer trying to punish someone from the past?

Or perhaps trying to save them?

Ripley's indrawn breath told Cage that she'd made the connection. Was Whistler gaining his revenge against women who could afford the opportunities his mother had missed? It seemed plausible. But they still had little hard evidence, and Cage didn't see Whistler as a killer.

Then again, what did killers look like? They didn't all wear white coats and stethoscopes.

"Can we see the roses, Whistler?" Cage stood and gestured toward the break room.

"This is about the hot bodies, isn't it?" There was a hint of fear in the young man's eyes now. "You don't think I'm the one doing it, do you? Because that's just plain crazy. I wouldn't inject hots into anyone." He stood and backed up against the far wall. "Why me? Just because I know how to inject an IV bag? Come on, ninety percent of the people in this building can do that."

"Nobody's accusing you of anything, Whistler," Cage said, though all three of them knew that was a lie. "We just want to see the roses."

"This is bull," Whistler spat, and spun for the door. Cage moved to intercept him, but the young man marched into the break room instead and yanked open his locker. He shoved an arm way back on the top shelf. And stilled. Groped around again. "Oh, hell."

"They're gone, aren't they?" Cage should've been relieved since he liked Whistler, but instead he was more confused than ever.

The young man paled to the color of milk. "I swear to you I haven't done anything wrong, Mr. Cage. I bought the roses for my girlfriend, honest. She collects glass flowers," he repeated with his hand still pawing frantically in his locker. "Our third anniversary is next weekend. You can call her and ask." He pulled out a limp set of green scrubs that might have once been wrapped around a trio of glass roses. "Honest."

Ripley cleared her throat. "Who else has access to your locker? Who has the combination?"

"The lock doesn't work, ma'am. It was broken when I was assigned the locker, but Mr. Dixon said not to worry about it, so I didn't." Whistler was looking younger and more scared by the moment. Was it an act or the truth? Cage couldn't tell anymore.

"Can just anyone walk right in here?" The censure in Ripley's voice rubbed Cage the wrong way, as though she was assessing his security and finding it lacking.

Well, he wasn't the one with dead patients, was he? On the heels of that uncharitable thought came a flush of shame, and Cage knew it was past time to get help. He and Ripley couldn't handle this alone. They shouldn't even have tried.

"Yeah," he said, answering her question. "There's never been a need to lock down Rad Safety before." He waved Whistler out. "You're on solid-waste collection today, right?" The young man nodded. "Get on with it. And don't talk to anyone about the roses or our conversation, got it?"

Whistler nodded vigorously. "Yes, sir. Thank you, sir!" He bolted for the door and the empty green scrubs fluttered to the floor.

"You're letting him go? Didn't you hear what he said about his mother? She fits the profile, Cage! Her illness kept him from pursuing his dream of being a doctor. And I saw him outside the chapel that day. He could've been in there with me. What more do you need?" Ripley was up in his face now, poking him in the chest with every other word, and Cage couldn't decide whether he wanted to kiss her into silence or gag her with the scrubs.

"Some hard evidence would be nice," he said, fighting to keep his tone reasonable. "And the last time I checked, being angry about a loved one dying doesn't automatically make a man a killer."

She curled her lip at the obvious parallel. "This isn't about you, Cage!"

"You're right," he agreed, taking her by the arm and aiming her not too gently at the door. "And it's not about you, either. It's about your patients and their safety. Try to remember that, *Doctor.*"

They stood nose to nose in the doorway, breathing heavily, until the fight suddenly went out of her and her shoulders sagged. "I'm sorry, Cage. That was unkind of me, and not fair. I know you're doing your best."

"We both are," he agreed, giving in to the temptation and resting his forehead against hers. "And if you're done yelling at me, you can call me Zack."

She sighed hollowly and looped her arms around his waist. "Zack then. What happens next? We haven't got another good suspect, and I don't know about you, but I feel like we're running out of time."

"Ditto." Cage kissed the tip of her nose. "I think we need to talk to Leo. Again."

"You think he'll listen now?"

"We'll find a way to make him listen," Cage vowed, but he didn't feel as certain as he'd like.

"I guess if he won't, then we go to the feds ourselves," Ripley said.

"Even if it means both our careers?" Cage lifted an eyebrow.

"Yes," Ripley said with solid conviction. "Even if. The patients' safety is worth more than a doctor's career. Isn't that what you've always said, Zack?"

He nodded, "Yeah, but—"

Her pager shrilled, interrupting. She glanced down at the display and he saw her shoulders tense. She swore, low and bitterly.

Cage's own pager was silent. "One of your patients?"

"No. Worse." Ripley stepped away from him and scrubbed a hand across her face. "My parents. My mother and father are downstairs in the café when I specifically told them to stay the hell away from the hospital."

"Your mother?" Cage asked, surprised.

One side of her mouth tipped up in a wry grimace. "Yeah. She showed up at the house last night after I made the mistake of calling her in a weak moment. Now they're both trying to fix my life."

"They love you. It's not a bad thing, Ripley."

The wry smile twisted higher. "They don't know the meaning of the word."

He caught her arm as she tried to slip past him. He could feel the tension humming through her and wished he could soothe the crease between her eyebrows. "Why do you insist that love doesn't exist? Why does the idea scare you so much?"

She jerked away. "I'm not afraid of much, Cage, and you're way off on this one." Halfway out the door, she turned back. "Why don't you come see our touching family reunion for yourself? That should explain everything."

Cage thought of the three missing roses, and of the fact that two were still unaccounted for. He thought that he needed to meet with Leo, and that he hadn't yet asked Ripley whether she would consider skipping the ballgame that afternoon.

Then he thought of waking with her in his arms, and of the fierceness of her lovemaking the night before. Of the certainty that she was taking each night as it came and rejecting the idea of ever after, which he'd barely begun to consider himself.

And he nodded and held out his hand. "Okay. Lead on."

THIS WAS A REALLY, really bad idea, Ripley thought as she snaked through the early morning crowd to a table at the back of the café. She should've ignored the page. They were in the middle of a crisis. Someone was trying to kill

her. She didn't have time for family drama. Calling her
mother had been a mistake. The latest in a string of mistakes that had begun the moment she'd laid eyes on Cage.

"Darling!" Ripley's mother stood for an exchange of
air kisses before she turned to Cage. "And who is this?"

"Zachary Cage, ma'am." He bowed over her hand and
Ripley rolled her eyes when her mother beamed.

"Oh, Ripley. I like him!"

"I don't," Howard Davis grunted from his seat at the
small table.

Ripley plopped down in a chair opposite him and
glared. "Well, that's fine because I don't like you very
much right now. Why are you here? I told you to stay
away, and I told you I wasn't coming to work at your
clinic. Why is this so hard for you to understand?"

Her tone bordered on belligerent, but it was sharpened
mostly by fear. Her father didn't believe in the danger, but
she did. If anything happened to him, she might never forgive herself. He was a pain, but he was her father. It was
that simple.

And that complicated.

In an insane moment of clarity, she glimpsed the guilt
Cage must live with every day. Then she felt him take her
hand beneath the table and squeeze, hard.

Across the table, her father looked somehow smaller
than he had the day before, and with a shock, she realized
he was getting old. New lines creased his face, and his
color wasn't good. Guilty concern washed through her,
easing the irritation and she asked, "Father? Are you feeling okay?"

He waved the question aside with typical imperiousness. "Your mother and I stayed up late last night. We worked out a few things, but she thinks that you and I need to talk."

Ripley felt a filial headache inch closer, waiting to pounce. "Can we do this later, Father? Cage and I are in the middle of something and I don't have time for an argument."

"I don't mean to argue with you, Caroline." The hated name flushed away whatever softening his gentle tone might have brought. "I never do." Howard rubbed an absent hand across his left shoulder. "I just want what's best for you."

The headache caught Ripley dead center between the eyes and her vision grayed for a moment. She stood, brushing off Cage's hand when he tried to stop her. "No, Father. You want what *you* think is best for me. There's a big difference." She turned to her mother, feeling a spurt of the resentment she hadn't even recognized before. "And what gives you the right to tell me anything? You taught me that marriage was two people with nothing in common locked in a big house together. Then you hired a cook and left."

"Ripley," Cage's hand clamped on her shoulder. "Maybe now isn't the best time or place for this."

She brushed him off. "That sounds like something he'd say." She nodded at Howard, who'd surged to his feet, clutching his left arm. She turned back to Cage and bared her teeth. "What are you going to do now, hang up on me? Or are you going to sneak out again and leave a note?"

Ripley was aware of the anguish on her mother's face

and the rapt attention of the morning coffee crowd. *Davises don't make scenes.* She turned away. "I told you not to come here, Father. Go home. I'll call you in a few days." She gestured for Cage to accompany her. "Come on. We need to talk to Gabney."

At first she thought the crash behind her was her father upending the table in fury. But when she turned back, all she saw was chaos.

Slow-motion chaos.

Howard Davis's chair was in its place, still bolted to the floor. But Howard himself lay sprawled on the tiled floor at the center of a growing, squawking crowd.

"Father!" She was on her knees beside him in an instant. His lips were blue. His right hand was locked on his left arm.

Idiot. She should have seen it. She *had* seen it, but the signs hadn't registered in time. "Someone get a gurney and call Cardiac," she snapped at the breakfast crowd, snarling when nobody moved. "Now!" She made sure her father's airway was clear and cursed when she couldn't find a pulse. "Compressions! I need someone to do compressions."

"I'm here." Cage nudged her aside and started pumping the motionless chest in the proper rhythm. "You breathe for him."

The actions were automatic. Tip the head back and pinch the nose. Inhale. Exhale. Count. Repeat. Ripley blinked back the tears and did her job. Inhale. Exhale. Count. Repeat.

"Dr. Davis!" Hands were pulling her away from her father and Ripley fought them, knowing she had to breathe for him. Knowing she had to save him. "Dr. Davis!"

"Ripley!" Cage's voice finally penetrated. "He's breathing. Let go." He tugged her aside. "They need to take him up to Cardiac now, okay? He's breathing. You did it. He'll be okay. Let the other doctors do their jobs now, Rip. You did it."

She nodded dizzily and stood, gulping air to make up for the oxygen she'd forced into her father's lungs. Her mother caught her in a fierce hug. "Thank you, Ripley. Thank you."

The sentiment was no more surprising than the gleam of tears in Eleanor's eyes, and Ripley watched dumbly as Howard Davis was wheeled toward the elevators with his wife at his side, holding his hand.

"Come on, Rip. Let's get out of here." The crowd blurred as Cage swung her toward the exit and bullied her up the stairs toward the dark, deserted halls of R-ONC. It wasn't until he'd herded her through the deathly calm of the outer office that Ripley felt herself begin to crumble.

"Oh, God, Cage. I almost killed him." When her knees buckled with the knowledge, Cage swept her up into his arms. She heard him groan as her weight settled on his bad shoulder, but the sound seemed very far away.

The sight of her father lying on the floor seemed very close.

Cage collapsed on her office couch with Ripley on his lap and held her close. "You saved him, Rip. You saved him."

"But I was so awful to him. And to my mother." She

tucked her head under Cage's chin so she wouldn't have to look him in the eye. "And to you." Hot tears leaked from behind her eyelids and she snuffled. "I'm a horrible, horrible person."

She thought she heard him chuckle before she began crying in earnest, and caught the faintest whisper of an answer.

"We're all horrible at one time or another, Dr. Davis. It's called being human… It's what you do with the guilt that counts." He paused and gathered her closer. "At least that's what I keep telling myself."

"No. ABSOLUTELY NOT!" Leo Gabney punched the desk in front of him as though it was responsible for the problems Ripley and Cage had brought to his attention. "This is an internal problem and it will be dealt with internally."

"Internal problem my foot," Cage snarled. "Your patients are being killed with injected cocktails of adrenaline and radioactive waste. If that's not grounds for a criminal investigation, then I don't know what is."

"Well, we both know your judgment has been called into question before, Mr. Cage. Didn't that judge in New York throw out your case for lack of evidence? Those doctors didn't kill your wife any more than Dr. Davis here killed Ida Mae Harris and Janice Cooper. Isn't that right, Dr. Davis?"

Cage rapped out a bitter curse and Leo turned to Ripley. "Are you sure this is what you want to do? Remember, if Boston General doesn't win the Hospital of the Year Award, I'm afraid I won't have the funding to continue to support R-ONC."

"Have you no sense of responsibility for the patients?" Ripley hissed, surprising Cage with her vehemence. Ever since she'd washed her face, checked on her father's condition and declared herself ready to face the Head Administrator, she had been quiet, almost passive.

It seemed she'd been saving the venom up for Leo Gabney. Cage felt a surge of pride when she leaned across the desk and Leo leaned back.

"This is a hospital," the administrator pointed out, shrinking back and waving his finger for emphasis. "Sick people come here for treatment. Some of them die. Our survival rate is one of the best in the country, and you, for one, should be very proud of that, Dr. Davis."

"I bet you fudged the numbers," she spat, before settling back into the chair beside Cage.

"Well, you'd know about fudging numbers, wouldn't you? The R-ONC radiation logs are proof of that." Gabney grinned slickly and straightened up in his chair. "None of us is beyond reproach, Dr. Davis. None of us. So I'll ask you again, are you sure you want to call in the authorities without my backing?" He cracked his knuckles. "I'd hate to see any of the publicity reflect badly on your father, you know, especially now that they've scheduled him for bypass surgery."

Cage surged to his feet, "You wouldn't dare!"

"I would and you know it. Boston General will be the Hospital of the Year, and the ten-million-dollar grant will fund the new Gabney Wing. But," the administrator held up a finger, "I agree that we have a problem that needs to be dealt with. Quietly. So I'll make you a deal."

Cage could feel Ripley vibrating next to him, strung

tight with fury and frustration. He touched her hand to keep her from exploding, and asked, "What sort of deal?"

"You two put on a good show this afternoon for the committee, and I'll contact a friend of mine in the police department and explore our options." Gabney touched his fingertips together, considering. "Yes, I think if we work carefully and control all the players, we should be able to spin this little incident to the hospital's benefit."

"Spin?" Cage barked, just as Ripley asked, "What's happening this afternoon?"

Gabney chose to ignore Cage's growl and answer her question. "Today is your day to take all the cute little sick children to the ballpark, remember? I've arranged a photo op for us, and a quick meeting with the Hospital of the Year committee just before the game. They'll be in the box next to yours." He flicked a glance at Cage. "Having a former Major League pitcher at my side will be an excellent touch, don't you think?"

"Bastard," Cage hissed.

Gabney leaned forward and grinned. "The committee chair was a huge fan of yours, Cage, though God only knows why since you only pitched a year in the majors. If your presence helps me win the Hospital of the Year, it was worth hiring you, even if you have made a bigger mess of Rad Safety than Dixon ever did." He flicked his fingers toward the door. "I'd suggest you two run off and get ready for the game. The bus leaves in half an hour."

They stood slowly. Ripley leaned down, but this time Leo didn't back off. She said, "If we play your game today, you'll call in an official police investigation of the deaths and the bodies. No more tricks. You'll call the police and you'll keep my father's name out of it. I want your word on it."

Leo smiled, victorious. "I don't care about anything but the Gabney Wing, Dr. Davis. You help me win that award, and I'll not only call in the cops, I'll let you keep R-ONC." His gaze hardened, flashing with a not-quite-sane light. "But if you screw me on this one, you're finished. Got it?"

Cage nodded and pushed Ripley toward the door. "Got it."

As they walked down the hall toward the elevators, he heard Ripley murmur, "And if I have anything to say about it, *he's* going to get it in the end."

Cage's lips curved. "My thoughts exactly."

Chapter Thirteen

"Is he awake?" Ripley lingered in the doorway, feeling unusually awkward about walking into a patient's room. Then again, the patient was Howard Davis, and he wouldn't be lying in that bed, hooked to a host of intrusive machines if it hadn't been for her.

"Come in." Eleanor waved Ripley and Cage into the room, beaming at her daughter as though Ripley was a savior rather than a horrible, ungrateful child. "He's in and out, but that nice Dr. Garcia says it's normal."

"I'm far more 'in' than 'out,' and Garcia is barely out of med school," a voice growled from the bed, and for the first time in years, the sound didn't put Ripley immediately on the defensive.

"Hello, Father." She stopped at the foot of his bed. "I'm glad you're awake." Then she found a smile, and maybe a shred of forgiveness. Perhaps they both should have tried harder over the years. "And you know very well that Dr. Garcia is one of the best cardiac specialists in the country."

"Of course. That's why I hired him ten years ago. Wooed him away from County General, too." The bushy eyebrows drew together. "You're being nice to me, Caroline. Does that mean I'm dying? Or are you gearing up to yell at me again?"

To Ripley's surprise, her mother laughed. "God, I'd forgotten how alike the two of you are." She stood and patted Ripley's clenched fist. "I'm going to take a little walk while you and your father chat." And she was gone. Again.

Ripley might have fled the room as well, but Cage's presence stopped her, as did the faintly ashamed expression on her father's face. Not to mention the fleet of machines he was hooked to, courtesy of her scene in the café. She took a deep breath, "Father, I'm not coming to work for you. Not now, not ever. I wish you'd understand that." It wasn't what she'd come to tell him, but the words burst from her without volition.

"I know, Caroline." Howard looked away, watching his heartbeat for a moment. "I think I've known for a while, but I didn't want to admit it."

"I'm sorry." She suddenly felt very small and very young, as though she had all of her life's choices ahead of her again.

"So am I." Her father shifted in the lavish private bed he'd installed in the Davis Suite, which had been built with his generous donations. "I just wanted to protect you from all of this. I wanted to keep you near me, the way I hadn't kept Eleanor."

The simple truth of it cut deep and left Ripley bleeding. She sagged back and felt Cage's arm around her waist, holding her up. Letting her lean. "Then why wouldn't you believe that I was in danger, Father? Why haven't you helped me?"

"I *was* helping you, damn it!" Howard's bellow lacked its usual vigor and one of the monitors bleeped warningly. "I was trying to get you the hell away from Boston General. Then I was going to go back in and fix what needed fixing. But I wanted you out of it first. Don't you understand? Nothing is more important to me than you." He fell back, breathing hard and staring fixedly at the wall. "Not Boston General. Not anything."

Of all the times through her childhood that Ripley had imagined her father finally telling her she mattered, that he loved her, she had never pictured herself wanting to murder him. But that thought was at the forefront of her mind. She shrugged Cage off and stepped toward the bed. "*I'm* important? *I'm important?* Well this is a hell of a time to decide that I'm important, Father, when my patients are being murdered in their beds. What about them, Father? What about my patients?"

"Ripley," Cage murmured from behind her, and she took a deep breath and stepped back, remembering it was just this sort of a temper that had sparked his heart attack in the first place.

But Howard didn't look feeble right now, and he didn't look close to death. He reached out and found the bed control, pushing the button until he was half sitting. Until he was capable of looking down his nose at her. "You're right, Caroline, and I was wrong. I can only say that I was trying to protect my only child."

"Well, stop protecting me and start protecting the patients who depend on us, Father."

He nodded. "What can I do to help?"

Cage sat on one side of the bed and Ripley on the other. And they made a plan.

OUT IN FRONT of the main entrance, the noise level climbed another notch and Cage winced as the babble irritated the dull headache he'd been fighting all day. Too much stress, he'd decided, and not enough sleep. Too much worry and fear. Fear that he wouldn't be quick enough to save Ripley one of these times. Fear that the killer would get her before Howard Davis was able to organize an emergency board meeting, eject Leo Gabney from his position and launch an official investigation.

Fear that once they had, his job would be done and it would be time for him to leave Boston General. Leave Ripley.

He glanced over to where she was herding the excited children onto the Tammy Fund vans, thinking that once this was over, he'd like to take her someplace warm and spend a week in bed. Sleep optional.

"Mr. Cage! You're coming with us!" The purple hair clued him in, though Livvy's wig was slightly askew beneath the Boston baseball cap. "Milo wasn't sure, but I said you'd come! You'll sit with us, right?" Every word was delivered at top volume, at odds with the silence from the wheelchair Livvy was pushing.

Cage leaned down. "Hey, Milo. How's it going?"

The boy smiled and touched the pitcher's mitt Cage had given him. "I'm going to catch a foul ball today," he whispered. "My dad told me they bring good luck."

"I'm sure you will," Cage replied, thinking the kid

could use some good luck. He looked wan, and if possible smaller than before. Cage walked over to Ripley while he tried to figure out who on the Boston team he knew well enough to ask a favor. "Is Milo okay to do this?" he asked once he reached her. "He doesn't look so good."

"The therapy will do that. He'll be okay for today." She touched his hand. "The glove was a sweet thing to do, by the way."

Cage shrugged. "I don't need it anymore." He glanced around making sure none of the hospital staff was in earshot. "Will your father come through for us?"

"I think so." Ripley said quietly, also scanning the crowd. Cage wondered if she felt it, too, the sense that eyes were watching them from all around. That ears were listening.

They were struggling against two enemies now—the person who was killing R-ONC patients, and Leo Gabney. Cage wasn't sure which one frightened him more.

"Father has people in the administration still loyal to him," she said. "Mostly they just tell him when I do something wrong, but I think they'll do what we need. If we keep Leo busy at the ballgame, Father's flunkies will have a chance to pull the records we've asked for and collect the hot samples. By the time the game is over, they'll be ready for an emergency board meeting."

"And goodbye, Gabney," Cage murmured. "Hello, new administration and an official investigation of all the murders."

A soft voice spoke at Ripley's side. "Dr. Davis."

Cage jolted, having not noticed the woman's approach through the crowd of wheelchairs, attendants and hospital personnel jostling for position in one of the three Tammy Fund vans. He relaxed slightly when he saw who it was. "Belle. How are you today? Are you coming to the game?"

"Fine, thank you, Mr. Cage. And yes, I'll be helping with the children today." Belle smiled at Ripley. "I'll see you there, I'm sure."

The final van began boarding, and the surge of the crowd carried Belle away while Ripley and Cage made sure nobody got left behind and nobody boarded a van without permission. With Ripley away and R-ONC deserted, it seemed unlikely that the killer would strike. They hoped. Because if they could get through today, Ripley's father would call in the authorities and the investigation would be out of Cage and Ripley's hands.

Until then, they played a waiting game. A worrying one.

As the vans pulled away from Boston General, Cage leaned into her and asked, "You feel it, don't you? Like we're waiting for something to happen. Like someone's watching us."

Ripley lowered her voice, reminding him that any of the doctors, nurses or volunteers around them could be loyal to Gabney. "What did you do with Whistler while we're not there to watch him?"

"I don't think he's the one, Ripley." He raised a hand to forestall her automatic protest. "But I put Security on him. He'll be doing paperwork all day and the head guard, Mike, knows to call me if anything happens." He glanced down at her, hating the tension in her eyes. "We're doing the best we can. If we can just hang on until this evening, it'll be over." The word *over* echoed between them. Cage studied her as she stared out the window at the passing cityscape. "Ripley, about what I said back in your father's room…"

She didn't turn, and he wished he knew what she was thinking. Was she sad he'd turned down the job Howard had offered him just before they left her father's room? Was she relieved? He couldn't tell when she said, "It's okay, Cage. I understand."

"He took me by surprise. I wasn't expecting him to offer me Gabney's job. And besides, I'm not an administrator." He wanted to touch her cheek, but their surroundings stopped him, as did the tense set of her shoulders. He was confused by the brief, strong temptation to take Gabney's job, to stay at Boston General. But what would Ripley think of that? Were they together or apart? He wasn't sure anymore, but he knew for a fact he wasn't ready to say goodbye yet. Not now. Maybe not ever.

"I said I understand. Once you've got Boston General cleaned up, you'll hand it off to another RSO and move on to the next hospital. Heather's death gave you a purpose, Cage. A motivation. My father didn't know that when he asked you to stay at BoGen. I'm sorry he put you in an awkward position."

Ironically, her acceptance ticked him off. "So that's it? Once your father takes over and the feds are in charge of the investigation, it's over between us? No regrets, no messy goodbyes, just 'have a nice life, Cage'?"

"Hush," she warned him when the last part came out as a muted roar. "It's not even close to over yet, so let's postpone the goodbyes, okay? We have to get through this ballgame and hope my father does his part."

She never looked away from the window, and they passed the rest of the journey in a strained silence. He wanted to reach for her, to touch her and make her tell him what she was thinking. But he didn't dare. He was too afraid he wouldn't like the answer.

The vans bumped their way into the lower loading area closest to the Tammy Fund box seats, Cage felt a swift twist in his gut. It might have come from the sure feeling that not everything would go as smoothly as planned. It might have come from the smell of the ballpark, from the ghosts of dreams that had died five years earlier.

Or it might have come from the sneaking suspicion that Ripley had said her goodbyes the night before in his bed.

He told himself to let it go and deal with it later, but when she stepped off the van and avoided his eyes, something inside Cage snapped tight. He grabbed her arm and hustled her into a nearby alcove formed by two massive steel girders.

"Cage! What's the matter?" She tried to peek over his shoulder.

"I wanted to remind you of something," he growled, aware of their colleagues milling a few feet away.

Her eyes snapped to his, and she must have read some of his mood. She licked her lips. "What something?"

She was braced for a quick, hard kiss that would defuse some of the simmering tension between them. He could see it in her eyes, and in the quick lift of her chest. But when he bent his head and feathered a soft touch across her lips, he could tell from her murmur of surprise and the hands that came up to push him away that she hadn't been prepared for sweetness.

He brushed her cheek with the back of his hand and deepened the kiss, feeling her fingers curl in his shirt almost unwillingly. He wrapped his arms around her, binding the two of them together as his tongue told her, *If we were alone, I would do* this *to you, and then maybe* this.

She moaned into his mouth and gave in, reaching up to twine her arms around his neck and offer him what he sought—the feel of them together, the taste of the thing that bound them to each other, undiscussed and perhaps unwanted. But unavoidable.

"Zack," she whispered, and she touched her forehead to his while their ribs heaved as though they'd run a mile. "This isn't smart."

He stared into the eyes that were so close to his own. "You could come with me when I leave. Any hospital would kill to have a good R-ONC."

She smiled faintly, though the surprise showed in her eyes. "I thought there was no such thing as a good R-ONC in your book unless it was a dead R-ONC."

His fingers tightened. "Don't even joke about that."

Pulling away, she rubbed her arms where his hands had gripped. She shook her head. "I was kidding, Cage, though it was ill-timed. Come on, we should catch up with the others. I'm sure Leo is looking for us."

"Ripley."

She turned back to him, but didn't answer.

"This isn't over. We'll talk about it later."

When she walked away, Cage cursed. They both knew she hadn't answered his question.

And she hadn't asked him to stay.

RIPLEY HAD ALWAYS enjoyed baseball in a distant sort of way, but this game was different. She was split in too many directions, and the tension hounded her, making her nervous and snappy.

Part of her wanted to watch the pitchers warming up and imagine Cage on the mound. Every time she thought she knew him, another facet emerged. Like the ragged, unshaven man who lived in a penthouse that would have stretched her father's budget, the confident, chummy ex-ballplayer working the crowd of men around Leo Gabney was a surprise.

Almost as surprising as his question had been. Leave with him? She couldn't and he knew it. She'd built her department from the ground up, and had hundreds of success stories to show for it. That was why she was fighting so adamantly to keep R-ONC open. She saved lives. She couldn't turn her back on her patients, and Cage knew that. Therefore, he'd asked her because he figured she'd never say yes. Once her father and the board voted to remove Leo, once the feds were brought in to deal with the deaths and R-ONC's future was assured, Cage could leave with a clear conscience. Damn him.

"Dr. Rip, is this the best spot?"

She glanced down at the pale, eager face and nodded. "Yes, Milo. This is the absolute best spot for catching foul balls. See how close you are to the field?" She helped Belle push Milo a step closer to the padded rail, damning herself for the compulsion that made her sneak a quick glance at Cage.

Leo had his arm draped across the RSO's shoulders—he was almost standing on tiptoe to reach—and he was expounding to the Hospital of the Year committee members about something. Cage looked pained, and Ripley was on her way to rescue him when the phone in her pocket chirped.

"Hello?"

"Caroline, where are you?"

Ripley gritted her teeth, reminding herself to be grateful that he sounded so strong, as though the heart attack had been nothing more than an annoyance now that he had something to fix. "Father. I'm at the ballpark. What do you need?"

"I thought you'd want to know that the board is meeting at five o'clock in my room." He chuckled. "I always knew I built this private suite for a reason."

Ripley relaxed slightly, thinking they might pull this off, after all. She was looking forward to giving the case to the police and taking some time off until the murderer was caught. Maybe she and Cage could take the time together. Her heart constricted. Or maybe that would make saying goodbye even harder. She frowned and dutifully repeated, "Board meeting at five o'clock. I'll be there, and Cage, too." Which would leave the kids at the ballgame short two chaperones, but it couldn't be helped.

There was a pause, then Howard's voice. "Well, I guess I'll see you then, Caroline."

"Wait. How are you feeling, Father?"

There was another pause, this one surprised. "I'm feeling fine. Your mother has been in and out, but I sent her home to get some rest." There was another chuckle. "It took some persuading, but she left eventually."

The softness in his voice was uncharacteristic, and it

gave Ripley a fluttery feeling in her chest. It had been years since she'd wished for her parents to reunite. The thought had seemed so impossible.

She cleared her throat. "You have everything you need?"

"Yes, of course." He paused. "Keep yourself safe, okay? I'll see you at five."

Ripley whispered goodbye and disconnected, hoping the glare of the sun and the brim of her ball cap hid the wetness in her eyes. *Keep yourself safe.*

It wasn't unconditional love. But it was a start.

This time, when she glanced over at Cage, he caught her eye. Their gazes locked and the energy pulsed between them, a living reminder of the night before. Of their kiss downstairs.

She had expected the passion from him all along. He had practically radiated it from the first moment she'd seen him. But she hadn't expected the tenderness. The kindness.

She hadn't expected that the idea of his leaving would fill her with so much pain. But she couldn't go with him, and she knew he wouldn't stay. He'd said as much to her father back at the hospital, but she couldn't, *wouldn't* focus on that now. They had to keep Leo occupied and give her father's people time to do their work at the hospital, while hoping to hell the killer didn't strike again.

The rest would wait.

He asked, "Everything okay?"

She nodded and lifted the phone. "Everything's set for this afternoon. We're meeting in my father's suite at five." The noise level peaked abruptly as the Boston team took the field for the start of the first inning. Ripley glanced around at the cheering kids. "I don't know, Cage. I have a bad feeling about being here."

"Yeah," he agreed. "I know." He jerked his chin at the far corner of the Tammy Fund box, where Leo was still holding court. "He's occupied, and I've got Whistler covered. But I still feel like we've missed something obvious."

The first two batters went down in quick succession, and Cage excused himself to kneel down beside Milo's chair. Ripley heard him say, "The next guy up is one of the most accurate hitters in the game today, did you know that?"

Milo nodded and touched his glove. "Guess he won't be hitting any foul balls this way, huh?"

"You never know."

Ripley caught Cage's wink and felt her heart turn over as he lifted the frail child in his arms and cupped a palm beneath the sagging baseball glove. She saw the man in the batter's box nod once as he dug in. The pitcher nodded too, and wafted an easy curve above the plate. The slow, fat pitch was just begging to be slapped into the seats atop the big green wall, but instead, the most accurate hitter in the game looped a high, soft foul.

Directly into the Tammy Fund box.

A cheer went up from the Boston General crew when Milo caught the ball with a little help from Cage. The noise was echoed by the crowd when the scoreboard screen flashed the boy's image, grinning and holding the ball up as Cage lifted him high.

Ripley remembered the angry, hurt man in her office

that first day who hadn't even been able to look Milo in the eye. And as Cage grinned at her now, she felt her heart turn over in her chest again and fall to her toes, returning on a rush of warmth and lightness. Of love.

"Dr. Rip! I caught it!" Milo waved the ball as Cage returned the boy to his chair. "I'll have good luck now!"

"Maybe your next round of chemo will get all those nasty leukemia cells and you can try out for Little League next spring," Livvy shouted over the quieting crowd, and Ripley winced. Optimism was one thing. False hope was another. It wasn't the therapy that was failing. It was Milo.

"Miracles can happen," Cage whispered, and squeezed her hand. "Just look at that foul ball."

"I have a feeling that 'miracle' had some help," she whispered back. Then, not caring who was watching, she kissed his cheek. "Thanks."

The next couple of innings passed quickly as the batters struggled with two very sharp pitchers. It was the top of the third when Belle touched Ripley's sleeve.

"Dr. Davis. You might want to look at Milo."

Ripley's heart tightened when she saw the boy's pallor and his exhausted sleep. "Damn." She'd hoped he would be strong enough to last the whole game. He'd wanted to see it so badly.

"I can have one of the vans drive us back to Boston General," Belle offered. "That way you can stay and chaperone the other children."

Ripley glanced at Milo again and nodded. "Okay. He needs rest more than anything. Take him back and call me if you have any problems, okay? The van driver is a certified EMT, so you shouldn't have any trouble on the ride."

She watched as Belle pushed Milo's chair down the shallow ramp that led away from the Tammy Fund's box, and wished there was something more she could do. The treatments were killing the cancer cells, but Milo seemed to be giving up the fight. He was too quiet. Too weak. She'd tried to get his parents to visit more, but they couldn't afford to make the trip as often as necessary, and their other children needed them as well.

It was a difficult, but regrettably common, problem.

"They headed back to BoGen?" Cage's voice in her ear shivered through her like a promise, but it was a promise she knew his heart couldn't keep. He wasn't ready to leave the ghosts behind yet.

She nodded and turned back to the game, pretending absorption as three more batters were mown down and the home team traded their gloves for bats. Tension simmered beneath the surface and she was acutely, elementally aware when he moved away from her at Leo's call, trailing his fingertips down her arm as if to say, *I wish.*

To cover the urge to turn and watch him walk away, Ripley glanced at her watch. Three-thirty. The day dragged. The urge to return to Boston General built.

The feeling of imminent danger overwhelmed her.

Ripley nearly jumped when the phone in her pocket chirped. Relieved to have something to do, she flipped it open. "Hello?"

"Dr. Davis, this is Belle."

The fear was quick and total. "What's wrong? Is it Milo?"

"Yes, I'm sorry. Nurse Lockheart asked me to call. His primary oncologist is out of town and you're next on the call list. He's sluggish and having trouble breathing."

"I'll be right there." Ripley snapped the phone shut and cursed. "I have to get back to the hospital."

"What's wrong?" Cage touched her arm and Ripley fought the urge to lean against him and close her eyes with exhausted worry. He was leaving. She shouldn't get too used to having him around.

"That was Belle. Milo isn't good." She cursed. "I've seen this coming, Cage. He's giving up. He needs to fight harder, but he's so little. So tired."

"With you on his side, he has no choice but to get better." While Ripley look at him, surprised by the uncharacteristic thickness of his words, Cage glanced around at the box crammed full of kids. "Come on, we'll catch a cab."

She shook her head. "No. You stay here and keep Leo busy until my father has everything organized for the board meeting. That's our top priority right now. I'll be careful, I promise. I'll stay in well-lit, well-populated areas of the hospital. No chapel, I swear." She touched his arm, feeling the unease swept aside by the need to reach Milo. "Meet me in the executive suite at five for the board meeting, okay?"

"Are you sure? I don't like this."

"I don't like any of it, Zack." She touched her lips to his. "I'll see you at five."

She heard him call, "Be careful," and she waved a hand in reply as she jogged up the cement steps and felt the doctor's mantle slip over her shoulders.

The cab ride to Boston General passed in a flash, and as Ripley swung through the doors to R-ONC, she was already running treatment options in her head.

Pausing at the entrance to the atrium, she shivered slightly, thinking that only five days earlier, she'd walked across the tiles and been attacked by Ida Mae's husband. So much had happened since then that she could hardly believe it. She glanced at the big clock above the café. Four o'clock. In an hour or so it would be over. Leo Gabney would be removed as head of Boston General, her father would take over the administration and call in the police, and the terror would be past.

And Cage would be free to go.

Hating the emptiness brought by that thought, Ripley hastened across the open atrium, feeling as though eyes were watching her progress. Feeling as though shadows lurked behind every display of a child's finger painting.

The nurses' station between Radiation Oncology and Oncology proper was deserted, but that wasn't unexpected given that R-ONC was all but empty, and most of the ONC patients were at the ballgame. Ripley poked her head into Milo's room. "Belle? Are you in here?"

There was no answer, and the lump beneath the bedclothes didn't move. Not even to breathe.

"Milo!" Ripley dashed into the room and slapped the code button beside the bed before turning to the little boy. She noticed two things at once. The alarm didn't sound. And the lump in the bed was a pile of pillows.

"What the—?" She was half turned to the door when the first blow caught her on the shoulder. She fell to her knees, gasping with pain and sudden panic.

The killer had found her!

The second blow hit her on the back of the head and

she fell forward into a dark, dark tunnel where there was no sensation, no pain.

And no way out.

Chapter Fourteen

He should have gone with her, Cage thought for the hundredth time as he paced the length of the Tammy Fund box.

"Where is Dr. Davis?" Gabney hissed between his teeth. "The committee chair wants to talk about R-ONC."

"She's gone for a hot dog," Cage lied, feeling dread curdle his stomach. "She'll be back any minute."

"She'd better be, or the deal's off," Leo hissed back through a camera-ready smile. "Got it? And while we're waiting for her to return, you can come over and provide color commentary. This game is about as exciting as vanilla pudding and the committee members are getting restless."

Cage was saved from replying when the phone in his pocket rang. He snapped it open, hoping it was Ripley. Hoping she was safe and had good news about Milo. "Hello?"

"Mr. Cage, this is George Dixon."

The ugly feeling in Cage's stomach grew worse. "Did you remember something else about the day you found the hots in the closet?" he asked, keeping his voice low and turning away from Leo Gabney.

"Not about that day. A different day." Dixon paused, then exhaled as though he'd made a difficult decision. "That wasn't the first time I'd found hots where they didn't belong. There was another time, maybe three months earlier."

Fury, sharp and edgy, poured through Cage. "And you didn't tell anyone?"

"I told Head Administrator Gabney. He told me he'd look into it."

Cage shot a black look over his shoulder. Gabney, it seemed, had been playing fast and loose with Boston General for quite some time. "Where did you find these hots, in the broom closet?"

"No." Dixon's voice was thoughtful. "That was the odd thing. I was doing top-to-bottom sweeps just before the regulatory board was due for an inspection and I found a hot spot in the chapel, of all places."

The chill hit Cage in the chest. Ripley had thought there had been someone in the chapel with her. She had been right.

"The chapel," he repeated aloud. It fit with the message beneath the broken rose stem. *Do not Interfere With the Lord's Work.*

Whistler's father had been a minister until just before his wife's death. Was there a connection?

Then, in a rush, Cage remembered what Whistler had said about the nurses who'd been in the hallway that day. *The short one who always hangs around with your girlfriend.* He had assumed that Whistler had been referring to Tansy, but Dixon had specifically said the nurses "weren't hot."

A short, unattractive woman who hung around Ripley. One who spent time in the chapel and quoted the Lord's name in conversation. The answer was swift and terrifying.

Cage slapped the phone shut and leapt over the low railing of the Tammy Fund box just as a good solid "crack" and the roar of the crowd announced that the pitchers' duel had ended with a solo home run. He fought his way through a sudden jam of screaming, waving Boston fans.

In the cab, he dialed frantically. "Pick up. Come on…pick up!" There was no answer in Howard's room and Ripley's phone bounced him directly to voice mail. Fear congealed tight in his gut at the sound of her recorded voice. Ripley never shut off her phone.

"Drive faster," he snapped. When they reached Boston General, he tossed a bill at the driver and was out the door before the yellow cab stopped rolling.

He bolted through the front doors into the atrium and slid to a halt in front of the waterfall fountain. The Cardiac ICU was on one side of the hospital. R-ONC was on the other.

In the parking lot, Belle had heard them talking about Howard Davis calling in the authorities. That made him a target, and he was helpless, trapped in a hospital bed.

But Ripley was in danger, too. And Cage couldn't lose her.

"Mr. Cage?" The hail from the security desk brought a flood of relief. He was there in three long strides.

"Mike, I need you to page Whistler. Have him meet you up in—"

The burly guard looked faintly ashamed. "I'm sorry, Mr. Cage. But I need you to surrender your ID badge and your keycards." He held out a hand, and Cage became aware of uniformed men moving to flank him.

Damn it! Leo had called ahead.

Cage spread his hands to show a peaceful intent, even though his heart was screaming, *Run! Ripley is in danger, she needs you!*

He'd failed Heather. He wouldn't fail Ripley.

"You don't want to do this, Mike. Dr. Davis and her father are in grave danger. I need your help. At the very least, I need you to pretend you haven't seen me."

The guard shook his head. "No can do, Mr. Cage. These orders came right from the top. It'll be my job if I let you into the hospital." He held out a hand. "Come on, now. Give me the badge and the keys."

Cage stepped back, feeling the indecision of the men at his back. He'd shared coffee with several of them. "Leo Gabney will be out of a job by this time tomorrow, Mike, and you'll be right behind him in the unemployment line if you do this." They traded stare for stare until Cage exploded. "Damn it, Mike! You've said yourself that Gabney is a profit-mongering hack. Why are you supporting him now? Come on! People are going to die if you don't help me!"

"I'm sorry, Mr. Cage." But there was a faint glitter in the guard's eyes as he came to a decision. "I'm going to count to three, and if you haven't given me your badge and keys by then, we'll be forced to detain you." He jerked his chin toward the elevators. "One…"

Cage spun and bolted.

"Two…"

He jammed his finger into the elevator call button, wishing the stairs were closer.

"Three…"

The doors slid open and Cage leapt aboard, only then remembering that these elevators served the west wing of the hospital but not the east. He could reach the Cardiac ICU, but not R-ONC.

"Get him, men!"

The uniformed hospital security guards charged for the elevators as the doors slid shut and Cage pressed the button for the Cardiac floor. He would secure Howard Davis's room first, then circle around to find Ripley.

He could only pray he would be in time. He wouldn't let down the woman he loved. Never again.

RIPLEY COULDN'T MOVE, but she hadn't yet decided whether it mattered. There was a bright light far above her and the rest was a blur. Was she dead? The idea brought a stab of regret.

She'd be leaving Cage behind when she'd only just found him. He'd never know she wanted him to stay at Boston General, because she'd never asked him to.

Someone whimpered, and it took Ripley a moment to realize the sound had come from her. Perhaps she was alive after all. Perhaps she still had a chance to ask Cage to stay with her. To love her.

When she tried to focus her eyes, the bright light stabbed into her brain. She turned her head aside. And the pain hit in a white, blinding wave that threatened to send her under again.

"God!" Ripley tried to clutch her head, but her hands

wouldn't move. Slowly, the world refocused. She felt a hard, flat surface beneath her, and straps across her chest and ankles. The back of her head was awash with pain, but it was manageable as long as she didn't move or open her eyes. Which wouldn't get her anywhere.

She cracked one eyelid and tried to scan the room, though each movement of her eye sent shafts of pain through her head and neck. Someone had hit her, she remembered now. She'd been in Milo's room and she'd been hit from behind. *Milo!* He hadn't been in his bed. Where was he?

For that matter, where was *she?* Fear shimmered beneath the pain, white and hot like rage when she recognized where she was. Treatment Room One. She was on the metal table beneath an A55 linear accelerator identical to the one that had killed Cage's wife.

"Oh, God!" The fear burned away the pain in a heartbeat, and Ripley struggled frantically against the cargo straps holding her to the metal table. "Help! Cage, help!"

"Oh, dear. What's going on here?"

Ripley hadn't heard the outer office door open, but she jerked her head frantically toward the soft voice. "Belle! Oh, thank God you're here. Quick, help me with these straps. I'll explain everything later."

The little woman, who suddenly didn't look as old as Ripley had always thought her, approached the table and clucked her tongue. "What have we here? These have loosened a bit. We can't have that, can we, Dr. Davis?"

"What?" Stupid with pain and concussion, Ripley watched uncomprehendingly as Belle tightened the straps across her chest and legs.

"I know you usually use those flimsy little hook-and-loop straps during your treatments, but I like these better, don't you?" Belle patted the sturdy nylon. "We can't have you escaping, now, can we?"

"Belle! What? Why?" The fear was chasing through Ripley in earnest now as she split her attention between the woman and the contraption that lurked above her like a giant metal vulture.

"You were looking into Ida Mae's case, that's why," hissed a very un-Bellelike voice. "Everything was going perfectly until then. I was doing my job and you were doing yours. Why did you have to stick your nose into my work? Why? R-ONC's death rate was still lower than the average. What did it matter that I helped a few needy souls find their final reward? Really, who was I harming?"

"The patients," Ripley replied, feeling sick and scared, still trying to align her image of a motherly, nurturing volunteer with the woman now walking toward the computer console at the front of the room. "You were hurting the patients. Ida Mae. Janice."

"I wasn't hurting them," Belle snapped. "I was saving them from long, slow, horrible deaths. In pain. Alone. That's how it ends, you know. Horribly." Her fingers flew across the keyboard, and before Ripley could wonder how the volunteer had learned to use the machine, it came to life.

"Ironic, don't you think?" Belle turned back to Ripley and smiled. "At first I was going to kill you with the stem of one of those crystal roses. I thought it would be nicely poetic and throw suspicion on either that pitiful husband of Ida Mae's, or on Whistler. He's an odd one, anyway. The hospital would be better off without him."

"Belle. Don't." Ripley tried to press herself into the metal table as the metal arm ranged itself over her body and the inner workings hummed.

"But once I got to know Cage and his background, and saw how he felt about you, I thought this would be far more appropriate." The computer whirred as Belle inputted a program. "It's all quite easy if you read the handbook, you know." She nodded and smiled, and Ripley thought the expression wasn't quite sane. "When I heard you and Cage discussing your little hospital coup this morning, I knew I was out of time. I missed you with the motorcycle last night, but I won't miss you with this." She patted the huge machine fondly. "Daddy never approved of women getting an education—he said it encouraged them to think they were above the station the Lord intended for them. But in the end, he let me take the computer and medical assistant classes so I could get a job as a secretary or a nurse."

She smiled benignly as the machine flashed through the first level of its warm-up. "Daddy understood in the end, just before he died." She nodded. "He saw that I was doing the Lord's work here, and he died a happy man." Then she glanced over at Ripley, and her expression flattened into a frown. "But you don't understand my calling. I thought you would—you're a doctor. You should understand saving people from pain, but you don't. That's why you have to be removed from the equation. You were going to ruin everything."

"Don't do it, Belle," Ripley warned. "If you kill me, Cage will hunt you down. He'll rip you to shreds and give the leftovers to my father. There has to be another way.

Let me up, and I'll protect you from them, I swear. We'll take care of everything and get you help, Belle. Just let me go!"

"I don't think so, dear." Belle shook her head. "I'm not worried about them. I've already taken care of your father, and I have something special planned for Cage. The Lord will provide for my work to continue."

Belle tapped a final key and the vulture's eye of the A55 linear accelerator began to blink as the little woman smiled a crazy, death's-head grin and said, "If you have any last-minute prayers to say, now would be a good time for them."

CAGE REACHED the Cardiac ICU at a dead run. The first thing he noticed was that the nurses' station was deserted. The second was that the door to Howard Davis's suite of rooms was shut.

And locked. "Damn it." Fear rocketed through him. What if he was already too late? Was Belle inside waiting for him or was she long gone? He tried to peer through the single window, but it was blocked by a "Caution: Radioactive" sign that shouldn't have been there.

Belle's idea of a joke?

Cage cursed again and decided he'd have to risk a frontal assault. Without thinking, he rammed the door with his shoulder and howled in agony. Furious with pain and worry, he clutched at his right shoulder and gave the lock three hefty kicks until it finally gave way.

Where the hell were the nurses? At least two of them should have been on duty. Even if they'd left their post for an unauthorized moment in the break room, the commotion should've brought them running.

Unless they couldn't run anywhere. The image of nurses bound and gagged in the Cardiac broom closet shouldn't have been so easy to conjure.

Cage gritted his teeth and charged into Howard's room, praying that Belle was in there at the same time he hoped she wasn't. If she was in the room, Ripley might still be safe. If she wasn't, then Howard might have escaped her notice.

Or else she'd beaten Cage to both of them and all was lost.

"Belle? Mr. Davis?" With no need for silence following his noisy entrance, Cage called the names and felt his gut chill when he received no answer from either of them. "Mr. Davis? Howard?" he called louder, hoping for an answering shout.

Something crashed behind a closed door.

Cage was at the door in an instant. He yanked it open and a silver trashcan rolled out of the small bathroom. Howard Davis, dressed and ready for the board meeting, was bound to the toilet with a pair of cargo straps. His mouth was covered with hospital tape and an IV bag hung from the medicine cabinet.

Cage took one look at the greenish-brown tinted liquid that had traveled halfway from the IV bag to the needle in Howard Davis's arm, and cursed. "This is going to hurt." Ripley's father gargled something, and Cage yanked the needle out of the older man's arm and flung it and the IV bag into the shower stall.

"You okay?" He pulled the tape and straps away and caught Davis when he sagged. "Howard! Are you okay?"

"Hell, no, I'm not okay." Howard's voice was weak but

it still carried the punch of authority. "Some volunteer gave me my meds, and the next thing I knew I was waking up strapped to a toilet watching something very nasty work its way toward my bloodstream. How would you feel?" He massaged his left arm.

"Stay with me, sir. We need to get you somewhere safe and I need to go after Ripley." Cage hoisted Howard to his feet and aimed him toward the door, wondering how the tiny woman had dragged the man's deadweight up and onto the toilet.

Adrenaline, he remembered, could help a mother lift a bus off a trapped child. He supposed it could do other, more sinister things as well.

"What do you mean 'go after Ripley'? She's not with you?" The old man looked around. "Where the hell is she?" He clutched at his left arm harder. "She's out there with *that woman* on the loose? How the hell did you let that happen, Cage?"

"I—"

"Freeze! Security!" Though he knew for a fact they didn't carry weapons, Cage was momentarily taken aback by the flood of blue uniforms that erupted into the room. Mike stepped forward and held out a hand. "We need you to step away from the patient, Mr. Cage, and come with us. Mr. Gabney is on his way to the hospital, and he wishes to speak with you."

"Gabney can go to hell," Howard spat, taking the words right out of Cage's mouth, though not with quite the same volume. "Do you know who I am?" He was getting louder by the moment, which Cage took to be a good sign.

"Yes, sir. Dr. Davis, sir," Mike replied. The guards did their best to stand at attention. "We're very sorry that you've been disturbed, sir."

"Do you like your jobs?"

The guards nodded quickly.

"Good," Howard declared. "If you want to keep them, go with Cage here and get my daughter. Anything happens to her, you're all fired, understand?"

Cage was out the door before the last, "Yes, sir," died away. He only hoped they would be in time.

"BELLE, YOU DON'T need to do this." Ripley struggled to keep her voice calm as Belle cursed and keyed in another command. As unobtrusively as she could, Ripley worked the broken rose stem out of her pocket with one hand. When it was free, she reversed it and scraped it back and forth across the nylon strap that bound her chest. Back and forth. Back and forth.

"Why won't this stupid computer…ah, I have it. Don't worry, I have it programmed for a narrow, high-intensity beam right through your heart. You won't die nearly as slowly as the papers say Cage's poor wife did. I like you too much for that." The accelerator, which had grown quiet moments before, hummed back to life as the glitch was ironed out. Belle smiled serenely at Ripley. "But even though I like you, Dr. Davis, I can't have you interfering in my good work, can I?" Cocking her head to one side, she said, "Then again, I guess you doctors wouldn't necessarily see my work as good. You only see your statistics, not the patients. You don't know how hard it is for them when they go home to their husband and

child with no hair and scar tissue where one breast used
to be."

She stood and stalked to the flat table to glare down
at Ripley, who quit sawing and closed her hand around
the broken stem, hoping it would go unnoticed. Glass
sliced into her index finger, but she hid the wince and
said, "Full mastectomies are rare for breast cancer." *Keep
her talking. Keep her distracted.* The mantra was the only
thing holding back Ripley's screams.

"Not back then," Belle countered. "Not when my
mother had the disease." She strode back to the keyboard
but didn't sit. "My father couldn't stand to look at her.
She'd been so beautiful before, but he told her she was
hideous after the operation and the chemo. He said she
never would have gotten the cancer if she'd been a better wife, a better person. The Lord had forsaken her, he
said. And when she got sick again, he told her to pray."
Belle turned back. "Do you pray, Dr. Davis?"

"Not as often as I should." Ripley sent a quick one now
as her fingers slipped on her own blood and the nylon
strap started to give. "I'm sorry your mother died, Belle."

"I'm not." The words were flat, though Belle's face
was still serene, almost eerily Madonna-like. "She wanted
to die at the end. She told me it would have been better
if she'd died in the hospital the first time, when she'd still
been pretty. My father and I used to visit her then, and
she was so happy when she was looking forward to seeing us. She was so pretty and he loved her. She always
wished she had died then, when she was at peace."

Women between fifty-five and sixty, Ripley remembered as her fingers slipped again and the glass sliced

deeper into her finger. Happy women who'd been looking forward to a grandchild's visit, or an anniversary.
They had died because they were happy. God. Belle was
saving her mother. Over and over again.

"Why the radioactivity, Belle?" *Keep her talking,* Rip-
ley thought as a few more strands of nylon gave way.
Keep her talking and keep sawing. She had to get free.
Had to save her father. She had to warn Cage.

Had to tell him she loved him.

"Why not just…help them on their way?" she asked,
sawing furiously. "Why contaminate the bodies when
that made it more likely they'd be discovered?"

Belle's watery blue eyes cut toward Ripley as though
judging her and finding her lacking. "I marked them so
they would be noticed at the Gates of Heaven. Father
always said that God had forgotten about Mother. I
didn't want that to happen to my favorite patients."
Calmer now, she sat back down and touched the computer console.

The vulture's eye blinked from red to yellow, indicat-
ing that the accelerator was almost ready. Ripley
flinched at the change, and the crystal stem slipped
from her fingers and fell to the floor with an incongru-
ous tinkle.

"Who are you?" she whispered, staring at the profile
of a woman she'd thought she'd known.

"I'm your savior," Belle whispered over the building
hum of the accelerator. "All men are evil, you know. Cage
would have left you behind soon, just like he left his wife
behind. You know that as well as I do. Now you won't
have to live through that pain. You'll die just like his wife

did, and he'll have twice the punishment, knowing that he failed you just like he failed…whatever her name was."

"Heather," Ripley whispered between suddenly parched lips. "Her name was Heather."

Above her, the vulture's eye blinked from yellow to green.

CAGE AND THE SECURITY guards charged down the hall-way, sliding to a confused halt when the chapel door eased open and a frail body tumbled out, clutching a baseball bat.

"Milo!" Cage dropped down beside the child. "What happened? Where's your chair?"

"Belle put me in the empty space behind the altar and told me to stay there," the child said, and his voice seemed stronger than usual. "She was acting all strange, kind of spooky. She left me my bat, but she took my chair so I couldn't go anywhere. She kept talking about Dr. Rip. I think she's going to hurt her, Mr. Cage! You have to go help her!"

Cage scooped Milo off the floor and handed him to the nearest security guard. "Take care of him." To Milo, he said. "I'm going to go get Dr. Rip, okay?" He hefted the bat. "And I'm borrowing this."

"Here." Milo pulled a white sphere out of his pocket. "For luck."

Cage took the ball and nodded, feeling a measure of calm return with the familiar feel of the seams beneath his fingers. "Thanks, kid. You did good, you know. Dr. Rip will be proud."

The rush of color pushed the gray out of Milo's face. "Just save Dr. Rip."

"I intend to." Cage waved the guard away and continued down the hall, carrying his bat and ball. When he reached the entrance to R-ONC, he stopped. "Stay here and wait for my signal, okay?" He waited until each of the guards nodded before he turned away and crept toward the offices, careful to stay below the level of the picture windows.

The narrow door leading to the outer office and the number of rooms radiating away from the main space made a frontal attack tricky. Worried that a startled Belle would hurt Ripley before he could intervene, Cage decided to leave the guards behind and go in alone. His only goal was to stall Belle long enough for the real law-enforcement types to arrive. With guns.

That he might already be too late was something Cage refused to consider. Ripley had to be okay. She just had to be.

The door to the outer office stood open, which was a chilling sign. Either Belle was already gone, or she was waiting for him. Cage was willing to bet on the latter. He straightened to his full height and stepped through the door, unconsciously juggling the baseball to a split-finger position.

The outer office was deserted. He was just about to push his way into Ripley's inner office when a familiar hum pulsed through the floor beneath his feet and Cage felt his guts turn to water.

Someone was charging the A55.

He was halfway down the hall to the linear accelerator room when he realized he wouldn't be in time. Belle's back was to him as she worked the computer keyboard like a mad organist. Ripley was strapped to the metal table, and the giant laser was stretching above her as the table tilted to the programmed angle in a mechanical ballet gone horribly awry.

Once the programmed sequence was set in motion, the computer kill switches were disabled, Cage knew. Even if he charged down the hallway and pulled Belle away from the console, he wouldn't be fast enough to stop the accelerator from shooting a beam of supercharged particles into Ripley's body.

The machine itself was shielded and double-shielded to protect the operators and patients from stray particles. But maybe…

Cage halted at the far end of the hallway. Neither Belle nor Ripley had noticed him. Both of them were focused on the A55, one with glee, the other with horror. He stared at the machine and blocked out everything but the small, circular port next to a blinking green light. It was the linear accelerator's weak spot, he knew from countless hours of research and courtroom testimony. A single blow to the sensitive area could disable the A55. Maybe.

Cage fingered the baseball. *For good luck,* Milo had said. And in a move he'd practiced a thousand times as a child and a million more as a man, Cage kicked and threw the ball as hard as he could, right at the imaginary strike zone. He felt the pain as his shoulder gave way for good.

And watched the ball curve away from the small, circular port and bounce uselessly off the A55's shielded cowl.

RIPLEY HEARD something thunk off the accelerator and saw, of all things, a baseball roll past. Her heart leapt into her throat with a sudden surge of hope.

Cage!

Belle heard the noise as well. She grabbed something from behind the computer and spun toward the door with a feral smile on her lips. Heedless of the drama, the linear accelerator changed its tone as it prepared to fire—directly into Ripley's heart.

"Cage! Help!" She jerked her body wildly toward the door, and felt the half-sawn strap give. She yanked again, hard. The nylon snapped and she scissored her torso to one side.

The laser bit into the metal table behind her with a hiss.

"Ripley!" Cage skidded into the room and ducked when Belle swung at him.

A filled syringe glittered in her hand. The clear liquid might have been as harmless as water, but Ripley bet it was much more. Much deadlier. "Don't let her touch you with that," she yelled as she fumbled with the strap around her ankles.

Belle must have inputted a repeating program. The linear accelerator fired mindlessly every ten seconds or so, though it was harmless as long as she avoided the beam.

"Hold on, Belle." Cage dropped the baseball bat he was carrying and spread his hands wide. "I'm unarmed and I'm not going to hurt you. We don't want to hurt you, Belle. We just want to get you some help."

She hissed, "Don't you see? I don't need help. I *am* help. I'm helping these women stay happy. It was all going fine until Dr. Davis got suspicious." She adjusted her thumb on the syringe and a single droplet of clear liquid glittered at the end.

It wasn't radioactive, Ripley thought. Maybe pure adrenaline. More than enough to stop a grown man's heart.

"Cage," she blurted, remembering Belle's words and worrying for him despite her own predicament. "Milo. My father…"

"Are fine," he assured her, trying to edge around Belle. "I got to Howard in time, and Milo is a hero."

Belle snarled at the news and darted her eyes back and forth between Cage and Ripley. Seeing that she was having trouble tracking both of them at once, Ripley slid off the table and moved opposite Cage.

"Stay right where you are!" Belle lunged, and Cage danced back. His heel came down on the fallen baseball and his feet flew out from underneath him. He went down hard, and Bell shrieked and followed him down with the syringe outstretched.

"No!" Before she could think to be afraid, Ripley leapt forward, grabbed the baseball bat, and swung it at Belle's head. It connected with a sickening *thunk*. The impact sang up Ripley's arms and Belle collapsed across Cage, who swore viciously.

"You bitch!" Belle slurred. She lurched to her feet and staggered across the room, holding her head in her hands.

She wove straight toward the linear accelerator, which whined with its recharge, preparing to fire again.

"Belle! Look out!" Ripley lunged for the disoriented woman and knocked her aside, feeling a warm breeze as the accelerator belched a stream of particles and fell silent when its deadly program finally came to an end.

And in the next moment, everything was still. Cage sagged against the far wall and Ripley stood staring down at Belle, who'd fallen to the floor beside the accelerator table. Reflexively, she touched her fingers to the other woman's throat. The pulse was thready and weak.

"Belle?" She turned her over. Belle's hands were clutched to her chest. Her bloody fingers were wrapped around the end of a crystal rose stem. She'd fallen on Ripley's makeshift knife.

Belle's lips curved in a sweet, satisfied smile. "Peace," she whispered on her last breath, and the lines smoothed away from her face. In death, she looked much as she might have growing up, before her mother's passing and her father's warped religion had turned her into something less than human.

And something more.

"Ripley."

She turned at the thick sound of Cage's voice. He was propped up against the wall, where he'd landed after slipping on the baseball. He was clutching his shoulder, and she felt a quick spasm of relief that he'd done nothing more than re-injure the pitching arm that had saved her life.

She knelt down beside him. "How bad is it?"

"I'm not sure," he whispered, and opened his hand to

show her the syringe. Its needle was buried deep in the muscle of his right shoulder. "You tell me."

"Oh, Cage," she cried, then bit her lip. Bedside manner, she reminded herself. Keep the patient calm and talking, even if it feels like your heart is breaking. "It's just a scratch," she lied, slipping the needle out of his flesh as smoothly as her shaking hands allowed.

"Liar," he whispered, and she could feel his heart thunder when she touched his throat.

"You didn't get the full dose," she whispered, seeing that the syringe was more than half full. "You'll be fine."

There was a commotion in the outer office, and a shout. "Is everything under control, Mr. Cage?"

He grinned ferociously, and she could see sweat break out all over his body as the adrenaline pumped him up to fight or flee. His pulse galloped at his throat and he reached for her.

"No," she yelled toward the outer office. "Get a gurney and a cardiac team down here, stat. We have a possible case of adrenaline poisoning here."

"This doesn't feel like poison, Rip." He drew her down and touched his lips to hers. He caught her hand and pressed it to his chest.

She felt his heart miss a beat.

"It feels like what you do to me every time I see you." He deepened the kiss. "It feels like being in love."

His hand slackened on hers and he sagged back as Ripley yelled, "Stay with me, Cage! Don't you dare leave me now. Don't you leave me!"

But she'd waited too long to say the words.

Chapter Fifteen

"Do you realize I only used this office for a week?" Cage asked Whistler as he loaded files into yet another cardboard box. "Not even that. I started here last Friday, and it's only Thursday."

"Not to mention that you spent Monday night and half of Tuesday being monitored up in Cardiac while the hospital was falling apart around our ears." The young tech held up Cage's lucky team jersey. "You want this?"

Cage shook his head and let the past go. "Nah. Keep it to remember me by."

A distressed noise came from the open doorway. Cage's head shot up and his throat closed.

Ripley.

Every time he'd surfaced during those terrifying, confusing hours it had taken his body to clear the injected adrenaline, she'd been there. Holding his hand. Cooling his overheated body. Talking to him. Then he'd slept through the night, and when he awoke, she was gone.

He hadn't seen her since, and he didn't like to think what it meant.

"You're packing so soon?" She stepped into the Rad

Safety Office and nodded at Whistler, who faded into the back room at Cage's gesture.

"New job, new office." He looked at her sideways, trying to read her thoughts in her face. Did she really think the words *I love you* meant so little to him? Was she so willing to see him gone that she wouldn't even repeat the plea she'd made as he was graying out on the floor?

Don't leave me, she'd said. But had she meant it?

"Right." She twisted her hands together. "Where are you going?"

"Not far," Cage answered easily, and was almost relieved when the interim Head Administrator poked his head into the room.

"Cage. Caroline. Everything under control?" Howard Davis was pale but composed. His bypass had been rescheduled for the following week, once the new administration was in place. Leo Gabney had been removed from his position with prejudice, but it wasn't clear yet whether he'd be hauled up on charges or not.

Time would tell, just as it would tell what shape the new Boston General would take.

"Father." Ripley rolled her eyes. "Why do you insist on calling me Caroline?"

Howard smiled and patted her hand. "It's your mother's middle name, you know. All those years, calling you Caroline reminded me that I still had a piece of her close to me."

Ripley's frown held little sting. "She's moved home, Father. You're going to the movies with her in an hour and you have cruise tickets for the month after next. You have *her* close to you now, so do you think you could call me Ripley?"

Howard scowled, but it was all for show. "I'll consider it," he grumped before turning to Cage. "You ready to go?"

Cage hefted the last of the boxes and propped it on his hip. His right shoulder still hurt like hell, but the sports medicine doctor had told him to hit the ibuprofen and come see him when the swelling went down.

There was nothing like a little joint surgery to usher in a new phase of his life, Cage had thought at the time.

Now he nodded at Howard. "Ready."

"What?" Ripley practically shrieked. "That's it? *Ready?* That's all you have to say for yourself?" She marched up to Cage and poked him in the chest. "You think you can waltz in here, turn my department upside down, say you love me, and waltz right out again without a word? Well, think again, Zachary Cage. I won't have it!" She spun and glared at her father. "I quit."

"What?" Howard Davis looked more amused than alarmed, and Cage felt a warm glow work its way through his chest and set up housekeeping in his recently abused heart.

"I quit." She repeated firmly, and jerked her thumb at Cage. "I'm going wherever he's going."

"What about R-ONC? It's your life." Howard looked genuinely perplexed now.

Ripley snorted through her nose. "You may have evolved, Father, but apparently not far enough. The hospital was your life and look where it got you—alone for ten years of it while your wife played golf. Well, that's not for me. I love the hospital, sure, but I love Zack more. If he's not here, then I don't want to be here, either."

Father and daughter stared at each other for a moment before Howard nodded. "If you're sure."

Ripley turned toward Cage. "You meant it, right? When you asked me to come with you? You weren't just saying that because you were sure I'd say no?"

The warmth exploded from his heart and suffused every dark corner of his soul. Cage grinned and dropped his forehead to rest on hers. He kissed the tip of her nose. "I meant it, Rip. I love you, and I want you with me. I'm ready to give you everything I have to give and more. I want to marry you and have children with you and spend the rest of my life loving you."

She closed her eyes and smiled. "Good. That's what I want, too." She turned back to her father. "I quit."

Howard shrugged. "Well, you'd better give your official resignation to the new Head Administrator, then. I hear he's a real stickler for protocol."

"You've hired someone already?" Ripley allowed Howard to usher her into the hall and turned back to Cage. Her eyes begged for his support. "Will you come with me?"

"Wouldn't miss this for the world," he replied promptly and followed them to the elevator, lugging his box of files. He could hear stifled laughter coming from the back room, where Whistler and the others had heard every word.

Yes, thought Cage, they'd make a fine Rad Safety Department. And Whistler would make an excellent RSO, though Cage was tempted to put the kid the rest of the way through medical school. He'd make a great pathologist.

Well, there'd be plenty of time to figure it all out.

Cage draped his sore arm across Ripley's shoulders as the three of them rode up to the administrative floor. He let his cheek rest on her hair and wondered whether Admin had a broom closet. If it didn't, he decided, he'd have one installed, just for fun.

"Well, here we are." She paused at the door to what had been Leo Gabney's office.

"Second thoughts?" Cage asked quietly, and was relieved when she shook her head.

"No. Just a big step, that's all."

"You have no idea," Cage murmured as he followed her inside the big room with its built-up chair and a panoramic view of Chinatown with a narrow sliver of Boston Harbor. The scale model of the Gabney Wing had already been demoted to the kids' playroom, where toy cars were now parked in the lot.

"He's not here," she said, disappointment evident in her voice.

Howard merely grinned as Cage dropped his box on the desk and sat in the awful chair. He leaned forward and touched his fingers to the desktop in his best Leo Gabney imitation, and growled, "Request denied, Dr. Davis. The hospital needs you here now more than ever, especially with the additional responsibilities your department will be taking on. I can't possibly let you quit now."

"Cage, this is no laughing matter." But her eyes glittered with the first spark of wary hope, as though part of her had figured out what the rest of her was afraid to believe.

He dropped the Leo act, stood up, and crossed to her.

"No joke, Rip. Your father is a very persuasive man. And," he tipped her chin up and kissed her softly on the lips, "you asked me to stay with you. Remember?"

"I remember." Her lips curved in a beautiful, mysterious smile and he was reminded of the first time he'd taken note of her, sitting in the front row of a Radiation Safety meeting, staring up at him as though he was everything she'd ever asked for in life. "I love you, Zachary Cage."

"I love you, too, Caroline Ripley Davis soon-to-be Cage."

This time her smile was blinding in its intensity. Then she frowned and Cage felt his heart sink. "What's wrong?"

"New responsibilities. What sort of new responsibilities are you foisting off on my department?"

"Nothing much," he tweaked the tip of her nose casually. "Some rich guy with nothing better to do with his money just donated a prime piece of Boston real estate to the Tammy Fund and Boston General. Your department is going to administer it for the families of cancer patients to stay in while their loved ones are receiving treatment." He paused a beat to let the news sink in. "Milo's family moved into the penthouse yesterday. Now that he's turned the corner, he should be able to visit them there."

"Cage," she gasped, delighted. "You didn't!"

"I did," he corrected, and grinned. "Want to go house hunting?"

He meant the kiss to be light and friendly, an affirmation of the changes in their lives and each other, but she deepened it unexpectedly, reminding him of all the things he'd almost lost two days earlier.

His life. The woman he loved. What more was there?

"Ahem." Cage resurfaced, blinking, and focused on Ripley's father. The old man stuck out a hand. "Congratulations, Cage. I think I've decided to like you, after all."

"Thank you, sir. That's good to know." Cage grinned and they shook.

Howard turned to his daughter. "Congratulations. I'm happy for you...Ripley."

She gave a little cry and threw herself into her father's arms. Cage stood back and smiled at the two of them, feeling his heart overflow with love. He reached into his pocket and touched Milo's lucky baseball, and as he did so, he felt the softest caress at his lips, as though a passing breeze had lingered there a moment too long.

We'll name our first daughter Heather, Cage thought. *Thank you for everything.*

And the air around him sighed once and was still.

like a phantom in the night comes
a new promotion from

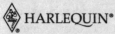 HARLEQUIN®

INTRIGUE®

GOTHIC ROMANCE

Beginning in August 2004, we offer you
a classic blend of chilling suspense and
electrifying romance, starting with....

A DANGEROUS INHERITANCE
LEONA KARR

And don't miss a spine-tingling Eclipse tale each month!

September 2004
MIDNIGHT ISLAND SANCTUARY
SUSAN PETERSON

October 2004
THE LEGACY OF CROFT CASTLE
JEAN BARRETT

November 2004
THE MAN FROM FALCON RIDGE
RITA HERRON

December 2004
EDEN'S SHADOW
JENNA RYAN

Available wherever Harlequin books are sold.
www.eHarlequin.com

HIECLIPSE

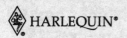

HARLEQUIN®

INTRIGUE®

and

B.J. DANIELS

invite you to join us for a trip to...

McCalls' Montana

Their land stretched for miles across
the Big Sky state...all of it hard earned—
none of it negotiable. Could family ties
withstand the weight of lasting legacy?

Starting in September 2004 look for:

THE COWGIRL
IN QUESTION

and

COWBOY ACCOMPLICE

**More books to follow
in the coming months.**

Available wherever Harlequin books are sold.

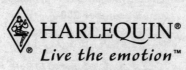

HARLEQUIN®
Live the emotion™

www.eHarlequin.com

HIMCCM

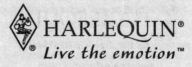

If you enjoyed what you just read,
then we've got an offer you can't resist!

Take 2 bestselling
love stories FREE!

Plus get a FREE surprise gift!

Clip this page and mail it to Harlequin Reader Service®

IN U.S.A.	**IN CANADA**
3010 Walden Ave.	P.O. Box 609
P.O. Box 1867	Fort Erie, Ontario
Buffalo, N.Y. 14240-1867	L2A 5X3

YES! Please send me 2 free Harlequin Intrigue® novels and my free surprise gift. After receiving them, if I don't wish to receive anymore, I can return the shipping statement marked cancel. If I don't cancel, I will receive 4 brand-new novels each month, before they're available in stores! In the U.S.A., bill me at the bargain price of $4.24 plus 25¢ shipping and handling per book and applicable sales tax, if any*. In Canada, bill me at the bargain price of $4.99 plus 25¢ shipping and handling per book and applicable taxes**. That's the complete price and a savings of at least 10% off the cover prices—what a great deal! I understand that accepting the 2 free books and gift places me under no obligation ever to buy any books. I can always return a shipment and cancel at any time. Even if I never buy another book from Harlequin, the 2 free books and gift are mine to keep forever.

181 HDN DZ7N
381 HDN DZ7P

Name	(PLEASE PRINT)	
Address	Apt.#	
City	State/Prov.	Zip/Postal Code

Not valid to current Harlequin Intrigue® subscribers.

Want to try two free books from another series?
Call 1-800-873-8635 or visit www.morefreebooks.com.

* Terms and prices subject to change without notice. Sales tax applicable in N.Y.
** Canadian residents will be charged applicable provincial taxes and GST.
  All orders subject to approval. Offer limited to one per household.
  ® are registered trademarks owned and used by the trademark owner and or its licensee.

INT04R   ©2004 Harlequin Enterprises Limited

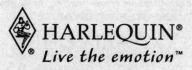

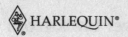

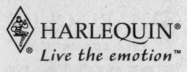